FROM ASHES

ELISE FABER

FROM ASHES
by Elise Faber

DARK

THIS STORY BEGAN when light transformed to dark, when elements were twisted into tools of torture.

Then it began again with a group of heroes trying to stamp out pockets of evil, a magical people learning to live in a world forever altered.

And . . . it began again with a woman who had a secret.

A secret that threatened *everything* she held dear.

ONE

Gabby

GABBY HADN'T KNOWN it was possible for a file folder to explode like that.

Papers flew into the air like a giant-sized version of confetti. Binder clips *pinged* down against the tile floor. And the Post-Its—

Her eyes slid closed in embarrassment.

The Post-Its were decorating the front of the LexTal's T-shirt —an abstract rendering that was more ugly Christmas sweater than Picasso.

Mason—said LexTal—didn't say anything, and he didn't have to. With his calm expression, his never-stationary gaze that took in each detail of the space around him, he was every inch the elite warrior who spent his life protecting his fellow Rengalla.

The Rengalla were magic.

Or well, they could *control* elemental magic. That along with the fact that they lived incredibly long lives—think centuries rather than decades—were some of the reasons they stayed hidden from the human population, and why they lived sequestered in small colonies around the world.

She was currently living in the largest one, aptly named . . . the Colony.

But names aside, for a long time Gabby's people had thought the biggest threat to their existence was humans discovering them. The Rengalla were a small people, could easily be overwhelmed by the human population, especially one bent on having magic at their fingertips.

But then . . . the Dalshie.

A much larger threat than humans, and one created of the Rengalla's own flesh and blood.

Because magic used for ill transformed a Rengalla into something evil.

The siren's call of the dark power perverted. It turned goodness into sociopathy. It transfigured, converted, *mutated.*

Rengalla became Dalshie.

And their corrupted brethren seemed to revel in nothing more than hunting down and destroying the Rengalla. Thus, the need for protection from a threat that was both internal *and* external.

A threat that had already touched Gabby personally.

The Dalshie had sparked the formation of the LexTals—the elite warriors who were the most powerful of their people.

But those elite warriors hadn't protected *her.*

"I'm impressed you managed to get them all to stick," Mason said, her thoughts having drifted so far away that she nearly jumped. Luckily, she stifled the action, oddly soothed by his voice. It was a little raspy, as if a piece of velvet had gotten scuffed, and paired with the most beautiful set of eyes she had ever seen. Green and gold and brown swirled together in a mix of colors that made her want to look closer, to stare into the complex depths of the man and puzzle out all his secrets.

He cleared his throat and her cheeks went red hot.

Staring. *Again.*

Mason had to know he was attractive, any red-blooded male or female could appreciate the chiseled lines of his jaw, the gorgeous eyes, the kissable lips, but she was the one with a staring problem. Mooning after him like a pathetic love-struck teenager.

Or a stalker.

Cool.

"I-I'm sorry," she said, standing and moving around the front of the reception desk stationed at the entrance of the infirmary. She needed to fix this. She needed to go back to her isolated bubble, to keep admiring from afar. That was the only way to keep her safe. Because if she let someone in—

Unthinking, she began to peel off the offending slips of colored paper from Mason's sweater in rapid succession.

One. Two. Okay ten. *More.*

She stacked the Post-Its together, realigning the little strip of adhesive carefully. Dear God, she would never, *ever*, practice her air magic in public again. She was a menace, a liability. A child had more control and—

"Um . . ." Mason said, and she froze.

Without realizing it, her hands had returned to removing the sticky papers and her fingers were just an inch above his . . .

A curse flew from her lips and she jumped back.

Mason reached down and removed the small blue square that was perched just above his groin. Turning it over in his fingers, he cocked his head, lips tipped up at edges, eyes dancing with amusement. "You kiss your mother with that mouth?"

Her lids clamped shut as shame washed over her. Her mother—

No. Not going there.

Her shame was because she was the first thing people saw when they came to the infirmary. She was supposed to be professional. Together. Not rattling off curse words and exploding folders.

Deep breath. If she just counted to ten, he would leave—

A hand settled on her shoulder and Gabby jumped so high she should have been attached to the ceiling.

"Don't!" She stepped back, bumped into the desk, and flailed. Her coffee cup rattled, porcelain against wood, and there was a series of crashes as pens and pencils and more papers fell to the ground.

Her eyes were open, but she couldn't see anything.

Just blackness, fear burning through her, freezing her lungs, seizing her nerves.

And then the hands returned, grasping the tops of her arms. Her body unfroze, but the blackness stayed, and the fear spun absolutely out of control.

"No!" She panicked, tore away from him, and she started to run.

"Wait. You'll hurt—"A firm grip caught her and held her in place. Words—*calm* words, she processed only distantly—filled the air. "Easy. Deep breaths. Slow and steady now."

No.

Not slow and steady.

Run. She needed to run.

"What's—"

Suz's voice registered and Gabby finally ceased her struggles. She glanced over and saw that the Rengalla's main healer, and her good friend, had come into the room.

Humiliation filled her from head to toe, heating her cheeks, making her shoulders dip, her gaze fall to the tile floor. It was heavy, stifling, and made her want to run all over again. Only this time it wasn't from panic, but from crippling embarrassment at losing it in front of Mason, in making a scene where she was supposed to be helping.

Why was she still like this? She should be over it.

She was alive. She'd survived . . . albeit not whole, that much was for damned sure.

Fuck. She'd panicked. Again. Her heart still slammed against her ribs, sweat was sheeted her body, and adrenaline coursed through her, making her feel both incredibly strong and extremely weak.

Or maybe that was because Mason's hands continued to hold her in place.

They were warm, the grip firm yet somehow still gentle, and making her yearn for something she knew could not be.

She tugged against his hold. "I'm okay," she said, her eyes flitting up to meet those pools of green, brown, and interwoven gold for a fraction of a second before darting away. "Let me go, please."

Her tone was calm, confident even. If not for the trembling that had seized her—the adrenaline letting down—Mason might have even believed it. But she was shaking like a leaf, and didn't have a chance in hell of convincing him that her roiling insides matched her composed tenor.

He scoffed. "You're not okay." But his hands loosened, and instead of releasing her, he ran them up and down the outsides of her arms.

He was comforting her.

Despite her freaking out, despite her showering him with office supplies, *he* was comforting *her*.

That made everything so much worse.

Her eyes dropped to the floor. "I'm fine," she murmured and retreated again, but with more purpose. Which meant that Mason either had to let her go or follow the movement.

His fingers slid free.

She tried to convince herself that she wasn't disappointed.

"Why?" He didn't need to expand on the question, not with the concern clouding his expression, the pity in his eyes.

She wasn't right.

And now he knew it.

Her stomach dropped to the ground. Of course he wouldn't let her pretend that nothing had just happened. Of course he would attempt to ferret out the truth. Of course he would want to know her deepest, darkest secret.

The single thing she could never tell another soul.

Gabby shook her head.

"Tell me." It was a command. One she didn't dare heed. One she, thankfully, had enough spine left still to resist.

Sort of.

Because his hazel eyes were dark and intense, and the way he looked at her, as if he could see to the depths of her soul, see the ice, the pain, and fear locked within her made her so damned tempted to unburden her soul—

No.

She couldn't let that happen.

"Suz?" Her eyes flicked to her friend, pleading.

The doctor was the person who knew the most, the single individual Gabby had confided in and she *still* didn't know the entire truth.

But Suz knew enough.

Which is why she gave Gabby the out.

"I need supplies," she said. "Can you get them for me? Closet seven."

A breath slipped between Gabby's lips. Seven was in the basement, and the furthest possible supply closet.

It might as well have been an all-expense paid trip to the Bahamas or an entire triple chocolate cheesecake for how much relief—and affection for her friend—poured through her.

"Yeah, sure," she told Suz. "I'll go now."

She turned and bolted out the door.

TWO

Mason

HE WATCHED Gabby disappear through the closing door, the tip of her blonde ponytail fluttering up into the air, and attempted to figure out exactly what had just happened.

Mase considered himself smart and competent, would say he was excellent at reading people, at discerning any threat they might present. But for the life of him, couldn't figure out what had flipped the switch in Gabby. Obviously, his touch had frightened her. But it wasn't as simple him startling her or coming up behind her and making her uncomfortable.

She'd been panicked, had begged him to let her go, and he'd wanted to—*God* he'd wanted to—but a part of him had worried she would hurt herself.

So he'd held tight.

That wasn't what bothered him.

He knew he'd reacted correctly, had made sure she hadn't injured herself on the desk or tripped over the clutter on the floor by lurching away in a blind panic. Instead, what sickened

Mason was that he'd enjoyed the feel of her soft body next to his, had loved the way she'd smelled.

The woman was terrified, and he'd acted like a pervert.

"You shouldn't have done that."

Suz's words were unnecessary. Mason already knew what he'd done was wrong on a number of levels—the most basic of which was that he'd upset Gabby.

"I know."

He bent, began stacking papers and supplies back onto the desk.

Suz placed her hand on top of his as he straightened Gabby's penholder.

"No," the doctor said, her voice fierce with mama-bear protectiveness, her golden-brown eyes flashing. "You have *no* idea."

"I'll leave her alone."

It wasn't something he should have needed to say. Suz knew his history, understood that he would never—

Pursuing Gabby wasn't even in the realm of possibilities, no matter how beautiful or sweet or deliciously curvy she was. He was no risk to Gabby because he wouldn't go after her. Wouldn't go after any other woman.

Because no one could *ever* compare to Victoria.

Thinking about or even the vague consideration of being with another person meant the possibility of marriage, of commitment . . . of children.

And he was never going there again.

"She's wounded," Suz said. "She needs care, not someone to make demands on her."

"I'll leave her alone."

Suz didn't answer, so he retrieved the last folder then placed it atop the desk. A curl of scent wafted up and tickled at his nose, and Mason swore he could practically taste the lavender and lemon smell on his tongue, floral with a hint of sharpness.

Sharp enough to wound.

He shook off the thought and opened his mouth to ask the healer to come to the gardens, his main reason for being in the infirmary in the first place, or at least that's what he told himself. And anyway, that purpose had been forgotten when Gabby had begun peeling off those slips of paper, had run her slender fingers over his chest, trailed them across his abs—

"What did you need, Mase?"

Suz *couldn't* have known what direction his thoughts had drifted. He'd worked damn hard to always keep his expression locked down, to never let anyone know the soul-wrenching pain that was still welded into his bones.

But the way the doctor studied him made Mason wonder if she had the barest inkling of where his mind had gone.

He didn't like that. *At all.*

"Morgan needs you. Francis was teaching at the Circle and one of the kids fell," he said instead of anything else—instead of the excuses, the denials, the blatant dismissal Suz wouldn't believe anyway. "A sprained ankle. He wants you to decide if it needs healing or just rest. Morgan stayed with him so the class could continue."

"I'll get my bag." Suz was already walking down the hall.

A minute later she breezed out the door without a backward glance and Mason was left in the empty reception area, files cluttered across the desk and a Hansel-and-Gretel trail of paper-clips across the floor.

With a muttered curse, he bent and picked up the small folded pieces of metal then righted the bowl on Gabby's desk and placed them inside. Unable to help himself, he began straightening the rest of the mess—organizing the mussed papers, mopping up the spilled coffee. All the while he tried to tell himself he was just doing what anyone else would do, fixing what he'd screwed up, and that the action meant absolutely nothing.

But as he straightened the small framed photo of a young Gabby with an older woman and man and carefully refilled her coffee cup from the carafe down the hall, it didn't feel like nothing. His heart convulsed and fear gripped his insides in a vice-hold.

Because . . . it felt very much like something.

THREE

Gabby

SOMETHING MADE her pause just when she would have pushed through the door to the infirmary. She glanced through the small glass window and saw Mason bent over her desk.

Her eyebrows drew together.

Then she understood and . . . promptly melted.

Because he was cleaning up. She watched him straighten the framed photo of her and her parents, tuck a few pencils into the holder on her desk, then pick up her coffee cup and walk down the hall to the break room, appearing a few seconds later with the mug full of the steaming hot black stuff.

And coffee. The man was getting her fresh coffee. After she'd acted like a lunatic, he'd cleaned her desk, had refilled her mug.

Honestly, there was no easier way to her heart than coffee and cleaning.

Her insides went a little gooey, her heart did a pitter-patter. And maybe it was a little sad that such a small act of kindness touched her so deeply, but she'd been alone for so long that—

Oh crap.

He'd turned for the door. The one she was standing outside of.

Her arms were empty because she knew that Suz hadn't really sent her for supplies and she'd expected him to be long gone. But Mason didn't know that. Plus, she was going to look like an even bigger idiot if he caught her staring at him again.

Fucking hell. Once again, why had she thought it was a good idea to practice magic in the infirmary?

Stupid and thoughtless and dangerous—

Stopping that train of thought because it was only dangerous if the man had been at risk of death-by-paper-cut. Or Post-It. Or paperclip. Or—

Focus.

Sighing and mentally shaking her head at herself, she whirled away from the door and walked—*cough*—ran to the nearest corner. This hallway was rarely used—a section of the Colony left empty as the Rengalla's population had dwindled—and full of shadows, so it should hide her effectively.

She'd just tucked herself against the wall when the telltale *screech* of the infirmary's door opening came.

It closed with a *click* and footsteps sounded softly on the wooden floor.

They got quieter and quieter until Gabby heard nothing.

A relieved breath slipped from between her lips.

He was gone. She wouldn't need to explain herself, wouldn't need to talk about the secret that threatened to shred her to pieces, the one that filled her with shame.

Waiting for her heart to steady, she pushed off the wall then turned back to the hallway that led to the infirmary.

And shrieked.

Mason stood all of three feet away, leaning back against the wall opposite her, his arms crossed, his feet spread. He looked both absolutely comfortable and completely dangerous. Forcing her breaths to slow, her heart to stop racing for the second time in as many minutes, the panic to subside, she began walking toward the infirmary . . . and, by consequence, toward Mason.

"Where are the supplies?" came his slightly rough voice.

A brief hesitation, her feet wanting to stop, but the fear in her mind and heart propelled her forward.

Away from him. She *had* to keep moving away.

"Gabby?"

She shivered as his voice flowed through her, and—God—she even registered the rustle of his clothing as he pushed off the wall and followed her.

But she would have known that even without the slight noise.

Her body was so in tune with everything about Mason—the liquid way he moved, how he seemed confident in every situation, the slightly golden sheen to his hair that separated him from his two identical brothers.

The sound just . . . made it real.

He was there. He was talking to her.

He'd never noticed her before.

She'd spent so much time watching him, practically obsessing over him, and he'd just now taken a second look.

Because she'd acted insane.

That was it. He was feeling protective. Nothing more. She'd triggered the overbearing, pushy, had-to-make-sure-everything-was-safe-and-okay gene that all LexTals seemed to possess.

So even though the faint rustle of his clothing may as well have been a train-whistle for how her body reacted, making goose bumps prickle down her spine and her cheeks heat, causing the spot just behind her belly button to clench hard, ratcheting up the urge to turn around, to throw herself into his arms and confess everything, he could *never* feel the same way.

Anywho, she digressed.

Because obviously she ignored her attraction . . . and the man at her back.

For one, Gabby didn't put herself out there. She knew it was safer to stay confined in the locked box, safer to appear shy when she felt anything but inside. Aside from her friendship with Suz and Daughtry, who'd all but cajoled and pushed her into hanging out with them, then to accepting their friendship, she didn't interact in any real manner with anyone.

Superficial, she had down.

The greetings in the hallways, the polite inquiries in the cafeteria, the smiles and queries in the infirmary, she had down.

No one would say she wasn't friendly.

But Gabby didn't give anything of true substance. If she wanted to chime in with a sarcastic comment, to make a joke, or tease someone she shoved that feeling down and slammed the trapdoor shut. And threw the dead bolt on it, just for good measure.

That was safer for her.

Safer for everyone around her.

"I thought you were getting supplies," Mason murmured, not letting the issue go as his voice coming millimeters from her ear.

She jumped, but only just barely. Progress, see?

Either that or she was just too damned aware of everything about this man.

Sighing, she said, "I think we both know that there were no supplies." Gabby didn't have the energy to lie, couldn't find it in her to going to add to the mountains of excuses that had filled her life over the last six months.

If she were normal, she could just ask him out and get over it —use the requisite three dates to get over her infatuation. If she were normal, then she might even be able to have a real relationship.

But she *wasn't* normal, so it was a moot point.

"You're new here, right?" Mason asked. He stepped up beside her, his long legs easily keeping pace with her shorter ones.

Gabby couldn't help but roll her eyes, because he really hadn't noticed her. It stung that she'd been so obsessed, and he'd spent half a year not bothering to recognize she'd been there. Of course the LexTals had been busy trying to save their people from the Dalshie, protecting the Colony after a major attack, building up resources to protect them from another assault that was sure to come.

Lately, the soldiers had been venturing out on one mission after another, trying to locate remaining pockets of their enemy so the Rengalla didn't have to be in such a heightened state.

They wanted their people safe.

They wanted to live freely and without fear of attack.

But that he hadn't even noticed her was . . . *ouch.*

Gabby lifted her chin. "I've worked in the infirmary for nearly six months." They'd reached the clinic, so she stopped and pointed to the bright red lettering above the door. "Speaking of which, I need to get back to it." The *hint, hint leave me alone* at the end of her statement remained unspoken, but she had the most disconcerting feeling that Mason knew it was there.

He smiled and it hit her with as much impact as if he'd punched her.

The man was lethal.

His eyes had always been her favorite part—not that she'd spent long enough staring at him to have a favorite part.

Lie, but a woman had to have *some* dignity.

Still, the glimpses she'd gotten of the swirling, ever-changing colors, the mix of brown and green and gold that was unearthly, beautiful . . . intoxicating had stayed with her.

She'd dreamed about those eyes.

Found their color matches in the mix of leaves and tree trunks and afternoon sunlight in the forest surrounding the Colony.

His eyes aside, she couldn't even save her sanity, nor herself from the attraction by saying the rest of Mason was beneath notice. He was gorgeous and of the tall, broad-shouldered variety. Practically cover model material.

And . . . way out of her league.

That thought propelled her into action and she reached for the door.

His hand stopped her, gripping her arm, tugging her to a halt.

"*Don't!*" She whirled toward him and Mason stepped back, raising both hands in a gesture of surrender.

"I just—" He broke off, gestured at her front.

She ground her teeth together—panic, shame, attraction, disappointment a tempest in her heart. "You just *what?*"

His eyes flicked toward her chest, and, for a moment, she got all tingly. Then her gaze followed his and she glanced down, caught a glimpse of blue.

There was Post-It stuck to her left breast, doing an impersonation of the worst ever pasty.

Perfect.

Anger, totally unnecessary and inappropriate, welled within her. She tore off the paper, crumpling it in her hand. "Motherfucker," she muttered.

Mason—the *fucker* in question—seemed amused. "Why are you always so sweet to everyone else and not me?"

"You don't even know if I'm new or not," she muttered. "I

doubt you've been paying me enough attention to know whether or not *I'm* sweet."

He shrugged. "I *always* pay attention."

So, he paid attention, just not to her.

She glared up at him. "Seriously?"

Another shrug.

Her hands plunked onto her hips, the Post-It she held in her hand crinkling at the movement. "You have absolutely no right to comment on how I act, you arrogant—"

He gestured at her. "Sure you still want to argue the point?"

Her arms fell to her sides and she sighed.

With her past, it was easier for her to be bubbly, to pretend to be happy and upbeat with those who just took her superficial mask in stride.

Mason, for whatever reason, saw through that.

Shaking her head, she turned back to the door, and her hand was on the handle when he spoke again.

"Why do you panic when I touch you?"

"You repulse me."

The words slipped from her unbidden. They were hateful, cruel, and so far from the truth that it was almost laughable.

But they were effective.

Because Mason didn't laugh. Because he didn't know they were a lie, and when she dared a peek over her shoulder, it was to see his eyes had darkened, his lips had flattened, and though he didn't visibly flinch, Gabby was somehow able to sense that the three words had wounded him.

Regret grasped her heart and squeezed. She wanted to apologize, to take the insult back.

But she couldn't. Her words had succeeded where she had failed.

They had distanced Mason and they kept her safe from his

questions, kept the truth that no one could know locked within her mind.

Where it belonged.

Where it would stay.

And since fleeing had become the only thing she was good at, Gabby grasped the handle and hurried into the infirmary. The loud slam of the door closing behind her made the cold emptiness that had for so long filled her soul seem even more stifling.

She didn't fight it.

She held tight to the feeling.

Because that emptiness was all she deserved.

FOUR

Mason

HE REGISTERED the *click* of door closing but couldn't care less. He was already halfway down the hall.

You repulse me.

The statement was a lie. It wasn't repulsion in Gabby's eyes when she looked at him . . . and yet—

No.

It didn't matter *what* she thought about him because. She. Didn't. Matter. *No one* mattered. Except . . . somehow *she* mattered. A woman who shouldn't even register on his radar, one who had been here for half a year (one he'd also deliberately ignored because from the moment he'd first laid eyes on her because he'd felt something inside him shift in that same instant).

Yeah, fucking alarm bells.

Because she was crazy.

Unfortunately, he wasn't much for lying to himself, even in the name of self-preservation, so the mistruth didn't stick. Hell, it didn't even make it out of his mind before it was ridiculed into submission.

With a muttered curse, Mason turned and headed for the armory.

Which was becoming more crowded by the day.

Dante, his boss and the leader of the LexTals, had decided that every Rengalla should receive training in firearms as well as magical combat techniques, so, of late, the practice range had been filled with beginners instead of solely the soldiers.

But the newbies didn't bother Mason so much as the Forgotten.

The Rengalla had existed in isolation for a long time. The Dalshie had been created, or rather the Rengalla had lost a number of their own people to the dark magic and its perverse draw. And, funny story, those who'd lost the battle between good and evil didn't go off and attempt to create a new type of cotton candy or to crossbreed fluffy and adorable malti-poos. They tortured. They hurt for pleasure. They'd horrifically experimented on humans and been party to some of the worst atrocities in history. The end result of those atrocities was a group of people—the Forgotten—who were no longer strictly human. Instead, they had limited magical abilities and longer lifespans. Logically, he *knew* that the Forgotten were what they were through no fault of their own—

Yet their presence still grated.

He made it his life's purpose to eliminate all remnants of Dalshie, no matter how small or insignificant, from this world.

And as far as remnants went, the Forgotten were a big one.

Memories—pained screams, black flames—surged to the front of his mind. They threatened to take over, to pull him into the stranglehold of his past.

Thankfully before they could, he reached the armory and the voices leaking through the sound-dampening barrier made of air magic, the interwoven sounds broken by the rapport of the shooters practicing and the resultant *thunks* of bullets bursting from their guns, hitting their targets yanked him forcefully out of the past.

But he didn't want to talk, and he definitely couldn't have managed to exchange cheerful idioms to save his soul.

You repulse me.

Swallowing against that statement, against the surprising depth with which those words had wounded him, Mason pulled out his earbuds and cued up a playlist on his phone.

It wasn't until the music was beating against his eardrums, a painful pulse of screaming guitar riffs and banging drums that he pushed through the door.

Inside, he nodded when required but otherwise didn't speak.

Taking up the last stall on the end, he un-holstered his gun and proceeded to empty magazine after magazine into the paper target in front of him.

Nothing else mattered.

Only the reverberation of the bullets leaving the chamber, the slight burst of sound that kept in time to the music, the rapid pulsing of his fingers as he depressed the trigger.

Fifteen shots. Reload. Fifteen Shots. Reload. Rinse. Repeat.

He reached into the pocket of his cargos only to realize he'd already used his last magazine.

Something hard clapped down onto his shoulder.

Mason's eyes flew down, saw the magazine, and pulled it out of the man's hand that stood behind him.

It was empty in seconds.

A pause. Another magazine found its way to his shoulder.

More shots.

Only after the last bullet was fired did he turn and face the man at his back.

Six months and he still felt guilty.

But Mason already knew plenty about guilt—enough to understand that it never truly faded, that once its iron-like talons had grasped your soul, it never let you go.

A *whir* signified the target being pulled forward.

The motor turned off with a *click* and he and Tyler stared at the paper.

Or the little that was left of it.

"I think you got it," Tyler quipped.

Mason felt himself smile. Somehow, despite the past, despite the fact that he'd shoved a blade into his own friend's heart, Tyler was there joking with him like nothing had happened. Being his usual flippant self despite the fact that Mason had thought Tyler had succumbed to the dark magic and had turned into a Dalshie, then had done his level best in order to kill him.

He hadn't succeeded.

Tyler wasn't a Dalshie.

And he somehow didn't hate Mason.

The world was a strange, strange place. *That* was the only reason he could think for why he played along. "There was a spider."

A grin. "Hate those bastards. Glad you killed it for me." A beat. "Pizza?"

Mason tilted his head, as though he were considering the offer. "You got beer?"

The skin around Tyler's blue eyes crinkled in amusement. "Always."

"Then I'm game."

"Good. Cody's coming."

Mason raised a brow. "Daughtry finally let him have a free night?"

"Are you kidding? Cody's the one who can't stand being

away from her." He rolled his eyes. "But Suz and Gabby and Dee are having some reality TV binge fest tonight and Cody was by himself."

"Poor guy," Mason said, but the memories of his own wife, of her own Girls' Nights—though they hadn't called them that back then—punched him in the gut. He'd lost her before there was television, before Internet and streaming platforms. But all those years ago, Victoria had loved going to the theater with the other Rengallan women, enjoyed having tea or going for a walk with her friends.

It was harder than ever to picture Victoria's face, to recall her delicate lilac scent. She'd been so sweet, so soft and feminine—

"You okay?" A gentle question.

Yes, *gentle*.

Tyler was too fucking intuitive.

Mason wanted to snap at him, but it wasn't the other man's fault—being able to heal psychically meant Tyler was more in tune with emotional and mental pain than any other Rengalla—but sometimes being his friend was annoying.

"How's that pretty scar on your chest?" he asked, deflection at its best. It was an air ball in a world of free throws.

Thankfully, Tyler still bit, though not in the way Mason wanted—which was going off in a huff. Instead, his friend fixed him in place with sky blue eyes. "We've already talked about that," he said. "I don't hold you responsible."

Which made . . . one of them.

Which was also why Mason didn't respond—only stared back and waited.

After a moment Tyler sighed. "Okay, I get it," he said. "You don't want to discuss what's got you upset." He lifted one brow, his typical cheerful nature making a comeback. "Want me to guess what's wrong and you can just say yes or no?"

"No."

"Great," he said, ignoring Mason and rubbing his hands together. "This will be fun."

Bastard.

Still, Mason felt his lips twitch.

"Spiders," Mason said lightly. "The fuckers make me sad insider."

Tyler snorted. "Nope," he said on a grin. "It's a woman."

Mason's hands convulsed and the sound of the trigger clicking made him realize that he still held the gun. After carefully setting it down—and cursing himself six ways to Sunday for being stupid enough to forget he held one—he stepped away from the weapon.

Idiot. Pervert. *Traitor*.

"No," he said, hoping that Tyler hadn't noticed. "It's definitely not a woman."

Hoping didn't make a bit of difference.

"Bullshit," Tyler said.

Mase's hands clenched again and Tyler reached past him to snatch up the gun. He pulled back the slide, glanced into the chamber to make sure it was empty, and a second later the magazine was out, the separate pieces were plunked onto the counter. Tyler smirked. "Just in case you were having any thoughts." A smirk. "Not that you should." He buffed his knuckles on his shoulder. "I'm brilliant and very good at reading people."

Too fucking good.

"I'm always having thoughts," Mason muttered. It was impossible to forget what was in his mind, even though he was doing his level best to try.

"Always having thoughts?" Tyler smirked again. "What kind?"

A sigh. "Tyler."

Ty gave a slow shake of his head, his smirk growing into a grin. "You're a filthy, filthy man."

"Shut up." Of course the fucker would make it dirty.

Still, at least the dirty meant that Mason was less focused on his brain and more on the idiocy that was his friend—who was now waggling his brows and making "ooh-ooh" noises.

"Give me the gun," he ordered. Surely he could scrounge up just one more bullet.

Tyler punched his shoulder. "Not a chance," he said, but at least he stopped with the sound effects as he tilted his head toward the exit. "Let's go. You need to shower before you're allowed to hang out with us."

"I repeat," Mason gritted out. "Give me the gun."

Tyler made a show of carefully stowing it . . . in his own holster, rather than Mason's before high tailing out of the armory.

Annoying bastard.

Still, Mason was smiling as he followed behind.

FIVE

Gabby

"I MISS THE WATERFALLS," Daughtry said later that evening.

Suz grinned and smacked her. "I bet you do." She waggled her brows. "I bet Cody does too."

"What waterfalls?" Gabby asked, forcing her attention from the so-bad-it-was-good reality show about feisty librarians.

"They're outside the shield." The shield being the only thing that protected the Rengalla living at the Colony from the Dalshie. Made up of special magic that could only be created when two Rengalla bonded on a soul-deep level, it was beyond powerful, and the Dalshie had yet to find a way to penetrate it. The shield was also beautiful—a mix of Daughtry's violet and Cody's emerald green magic, the strands were woven together like an expensive tapestry.

"Everything good is outside the shield," Suz muttered, but Gabby knew the healer's complaint was less about actual complaining and more about the fact that they'd spent too long on high alert.

The Rengalla had been in a constant state of fear.

Would they be attacked? Would someone lose their battle against the temptation of the dark magic and devastate them from the inside out?

Something had to change.

But right now there weren't any good solutions aside from pulling everyone into the Colonies and doing their best to keep them safe.

So they stayed.

So they waited.

So . . . they went a little stir crazy.

Except for Gabby.

For the first time in her life, she had friends and felt like she was part of something.

Dee sighed, pulling Gabby out of her own head. "I only disagree with you a little bit."

"That's because Cody's usually on the inside of the shield with you." Another mutter from Suz, and Gabby couldn't deny that she also felt a little jealous of her friend and the fact that she'd found someone who shared her life in such a meaningful way. It made Gabby ache, though she was happy that Dee had found someone to love her. Her friend deserved to have everything.

"True." Dee smiled. "But when everything calms down, I'll show them to you. The actual falls are quite beautiful. The water rushes by incredibly fast and not only can you feel it in vibrating through your stomach, but you can actually walk right up to their edge. Cody took me there before we had to shrink the shield."

Suz snorted, but Gabby was entranced. "Are they really loud? And big?" She'd never seen a waterfall, not outside of a book, that was.

"Not huge," Dee said. "But still pretty impressive. When it's safe we'll go."

"I'd like that," Gabby said and snagged Suz's popcorn. "How's *your* man?" she asked the doctor.

Suz scowled. "He's not *my* man." She grabbed the bowl back even as her face softened. "But he's fine. And speaking of men, did you see the sad look on your bondmate's face when we kicked him out of here, Dee? Downtrodden puppies had nothing on Cody."

They laughed even as Daughtry got the slightly glazed-over look on her face that Suz had recently dubbed as "Cody drunk." It happened every time Daughtry and Cody were communicating along their bond.

With a groan, Suz turned to Gabby. "We've done it now. Pretty soon Dee will be blushing and shooing us out of here so that she and Cody can get their friskies on."

"Never!" Dee said even as her cheeks went beet red, which, of course, made Gabby and Suz burst into hysterical giggles that Daughtry was hard-pressed to ignore. Eventually they were all laughing, unable to hear the show and not caring in the least.

"What did Cody want?" Gabby asked once they were in control of themselves again.

Daughtry smiled and her violet eyes went soft. "Oh, he was just saying he missed me—"

"And asking how soon he could come back," Suz interjected. She turned to Gabby. "It's always so much worse for the guy in a bonded relationship." A shrug. "Or at least, that's what my records say." Bonding was rare, and had gotten rarer over the years, until Dee and Cody were the first bonded pair in centuries. "The man gets all manly and animalistic and possessive, and needs to check and make sure his maiden is locked up in the tower."

"Oh, shut up." Dee smacked Suz's arm. "He does *not*."

Silence.

Because Cody was nothing if not possessive, and he was also a LexTal, which meant he put the P in protective as well.

"Fine." Dee huffed. "He *can* be a little overprotective, but I'm protective of him right back." A shrug. "Plus, I happen to like it when Cody gets all animalistic. *Rawr*." Daughtry pretended to have claws, cackling when Gabby and Suz gagged. "Okay. Fine, Suz. You're right," Dee said once they'd stopped. "He *was* asking how soon he could come back. Doesn't matter though. He's with Tyler, John, and Morgan watching a game. They even convinced Mason to grab a beer with them, so they won't let Cody leave for a while. We can binge more librarians!" She shoved a chocolate into her mouth. "Sports, blegh," she mumbled around the mouthful. "How can that compare with overdue library books and stock-room drama?"

Gabby chuckled even as her mind spun. Just hearing Mason's name did something to her insides, made them both squishy and alert. She wanted to ask about him, even when she knew she shouldn't.

"What's his deal anyway?" she blurted.

Apparently *shouldn't* didn't matter when it came to her fascination with Mason.

"Who's deal?" Daughtry asked.

Suz didn't need clarification. Her golden-brown eyes were too perceptive. "Mason is a good man," she said, fixing Gabby in place with her stare. "But he's had a difficult time of it. His wife and son were murdered by the Dalshie. He's broken, hun. Not someone you should let yourself be interested in. He—" Her expression went sad. "I think that part of him is well and truly shattered, and will always remain that way."

Daughtry gasped. Gabby's shock was quieter but no less heart wrenching. The poor man. Too have lost so much—

"How awful," Dee said.

"It was a long time ago," Suz replied. "But . . ."

"Someone doesn't just get over that," Gabby said, her own pain, her own dark memories blatant reminders of that fact.

Suz held her eyes and nodded. "Exactly."

A burst of noise from the TV drew their attention. They watched as a fight broke out and books started flying. Daughtry made a light comment about that being sacrilegious and the tension broke. Still, they were subdued and—except for the occasional snarky comment regarding a character they despised —they watched the show in silence.

Gabby's silence came from being lost in thought about Mason, about what he'd suffered, and how someone could survive that. Which got her thinking about Daughtry and how Dee was bonded telepathically with Cody. What would happen to the other if they were separated, if one of them died? Loss was hard enough, but to be so connected to a person and *then* lose them?

That was a terrifying thought.

"Dee?" She bit her lip, wanting to ask but scared it might hurt her friend.

"What is it?" Daughtry asked, pausing the show and setting the remote down.

"I—" Gabby shook her head. "Never mind. I'm being nosy."

Dee smiled. "You mean you're being a Rengalla, since being nosy is pretty much in our DNA." She nudged Gabby's shoulder. "Ask me. I'm an open book."

"I was just . . ." Gabby wrinkled her nose, sighed. "I was just wondering about bonding. I mean, I know you and Cody can communicate telepathically, but what does the bond actually mean? What does it do?"

"I wish I understood it completely," Dee said. "I have the book on Bond Magic, but it talks more about what we can do with our powers than why bonding exists in the first place."

"But . . . the Rengalla—I mean, *we're*—" Gabby bit her lip, hating she'd almost revealed something that shouldn't be revealed. She wasn't a normal Rengalla, didn't consider herself one in a lot of ways, considering how she'd grown up. But these were dangerous times with the Dalshie hovering at the gate and Gabby couldn't afford for anyone to know.

No one could know.

She shrugged. "We're big on records and books," she finished lamely. "Can't you just look it up? Or ask another bonded couple?"

Dee smiled ruefully. "A lot of the bond information was destroyed by the former Council"—leaders of the Rengalla who'd been infiltrated by the Dalshie—"and as far as I can tell, the book I have and the records from past healers Suz has in infirmary is the extent of knowledge remaining."

"And," Suz said. "I've used the records to tried to locate every bonded couple in my registry, but many of them are older and isolated and nearly impossible to reach. Or—" She broke off and Gabby read between the lines. Either they eschewed email and cell phones and had moved, not bothering to update their information with the Colony . . . or something bad had happened to them. "I've even reached out to those Rengalla whose parents or grandparents had recorded bonds," she said softly, "but the bonding between Cody and Dee was the first in almost five hundred years."

Gabby blinked. She hadn't realized it had been that long. "Wow."

"So no one to talk to, and the only useful thing I have is Suz's records declaring Cody a possessive beast." Dee huffed. "And a book I can barely decipher."

"What do you mean?"

Another huff. "The only thing the book I've been able to make heads or tails of is that supposedly a bond's purpose is to increase our 'offspring's' power." She rolled her eyes. "Like the only thing I'm good for is being a freaking magical incubator or something."

Gabby snorted.

Dee flashed her a smile before sobering. "I just think there has to be more to it than creating Rengalla with stronger magic—"

"Dear God," Suz said, interrupting her. "I just had the image of tiny Daughtrys running down the hall whipping violet strands of magic around. We just got the place back together after your last magical exploding shenanigans, give me some time before I have to start considering your spawn coming into the picture and destroying it."

"First," Dee pointed out. "The exploding was because of the Dalshie—or well, me trying to protect myself from the Dalshie."

"Po-tay-to, Po-tah-to," Suz teased.

"Plus, you love kids," Dee said, adding with a slightly evil grin, "But, rest assured, if Cody and I ever get to the point where we're ready for little magical geniuses, you'll be the first to know."

"Don't remind me." Suz groaned even as Gabby laughed. "Being the birth control guru amongst the Rengalla is already uncomfortable enough."

But the doctor was grinning.

They all laughed, but then Dee sobered and grabbed Gabby's hand. "The bond is the best thing that has ever happened to me," she said. "I mean, don't get me wrong — there *are* drawbacks. Privacy is an issue because your thoughts are never *only* your own again." A shrug. "But Cody and I are working on that, on building some layers of privacy between our minds. Still, even if that doesn't work, the intimacy, the connection, the *soul-deep* link to the man I love is worth it any loss of privacy."

Gabby's breath caught as she was hit with such a pang of longing that it actually hurt. Because the terror of being so closely tied to someone aside, she wanted what Daughtry and Cody had.

Connection. Love. Acceptance.

But as much as she might want it, Gabby knew she would never have it.

With her past, her secrets, it would be impossible to ever allow herself to get so close to someone.

"Ugh." Gabby jumped when Suz groaned. "Enough of this true love stuff," she grumbled. "This is supposed to be a Girl's Night. I need more TV and chocolate."

"Well *birth control guru*," Dee said with a grin. "That was the last episode of *When Librarians Attack*. It's your turn to pick the next show."

"Yes!" Suz snagged up the remote. "Time for *Wedding Dresses from Hell*."

Gabby and Daughtry made a few obligatory comments about poor quality television—they had to pretend to have *some* taste—but neither of them protested when Suz cued up the show, the thumbnail a garish pink and fluorescent orange confection overwhelming a petite bride. Instead, they shared a grin, grabbed their snacks, and settled in for the ride.

As the show played and the drama ensued, Gabby thought she was lucky to have such good friends.

Once she would have never thought it possible to have people accept her, to enjoy a quiet night like this.

Things had changed.

Yet, she knew that deep-down, they hadn't changed enough.

Because if anyone found out the full truth, she would lose everything.

A FEW DAYS LATER, Gabby stared at her hands and listened to the excited murmuring of the students around her. She was in the gardens, surrounded by the freshly replanted grove of pine trees.

he gardens were magazine-perfect.

Then again everything in the Colony was.

And Gabby, a girl who'd grown up in a rusted, falling apart double-wide, with Formica countertops and a shower that was one step shy of ice cold on its best days, never felt more ill at ease then when surrounded by luxury. So while the gardens didn't have the crystal chandeliers and chocolate hardwood floors, nor the marble and bronze finishes that populated the rest of the Colony's design, they were still nice enough to make her feel uncomfortable.

It wasn't nature or even the trees that did so.

The winding, sun-dappled paths brought contentment. But the main gathering spot—the clearing dubbed the Circle with its Colorado lodge feel—did. A humongous slate-covered fire pit sat in the center encircled by benches, each sanded so fiercely that their finish was velvet soft. Add in the cashmere throws and silk pillows and—

At least Francis, her instructor, seemed to not be swayed by such details. She, along with every other student in the class, sat on hard-as-nails upturned logs in a small clearing just around the bend from the adult's gathering spot. Cashmere and fire pits weren't welcome *here*, only textbooks and questions.

It was such a departure from the Colony's normal furnishings that Gabby had initially been shocked. Until she'd understood the purpose.

Ignoring discomfort to focus on magic had been the first lesson Francis had taught them.

It was an important one. Because magic was often conducted under stressful, or at least distracting, circumstances. If the Rengalla couldn't even ignore an aching bottom in order to use their powers, then they would be in trouble if the Dalshie ever decided to attack again or if they had to act in a hurry.

A giggle drew Gabby's focus. She glanced over to see two boys poking each other and laughing like it was the most hilarious experience on earth.

She didn't find it amusing.

Of course she was also a good twenty years older than any other student in the clearing.

There was nothing quite as humiliating as being in a class filled with six and seven-year-olds. But since Gabby hadn't grown up in the Colony, she didn't have any magical education to speak of.

So she was starting at the beginning.

Billy Madison had nothing on her.

Dee had insisted on showing her the so-bad-it-was-good comedy the night before, and Gabby couldn't ignore the similarities. A grown up in children's classes. A *failing* grown up in them.

Le sigh.

But she digressed.

She was putting her pride aside and ignoring her ego to focus on what was important. She needed to learn the basics, and that began at primary—or elemental—magic. The first tier of magic involved manipulating a single element—earth, wind, water, or fire.

Not that she seemed to be showing an iota of aptitude for controlling *anything*.

Six-year-old Daniel was better at it than her, and his powers had only manifested mere weeks before.

There was a swell of noise—kids hurrying to get their last bit of conversation in before instruction began—and Gabby shifted her gaze from the boys to the trees. Francis emerged from the shadowed path and walked toward them.

He wore jeans and a pale blue sweater, and his shiny black boots gleamed in the sunlight. His hair was an ashy blond laced with patches of gray at his temples.

Francis appeared to be about sixty human years but was probably ten times that, and though he'd been a patient teacher, Gabby knew she was getting on his nerves. She wasn't progressing, and younger students were flying past her at regular intervals.

Gabby knew why.

She just hadn't mustered the strength yet to take the leap and move beyond the fear.

If that leap went wrong and someone found out the truth about her past, everything she'd worked to establish could disappear in a heartbeat.

Part of her felt that because Francis was the oldest Rengalla by far—rumor had it he'd rubbed elbows with da Vinci—there wasn't anything she could tell him that would shock him.

The rest of her was too afraid.

"Hello, children," he said then added with a smile, "And Gabby."

"Hello, professor," they all dutifully replied back.

"Last week we began working on air. Today we will continue the lesson. Pair up and practice conjuring small spheres of air. Go." He waited until they'd rearranged themselves into groups of two before he spoke again. "Remember to keep the balls small—control is very important. Now practice gathering your magic in your mind and releasing it. Then when you're ready, your partner will try to push the sphere out of your grasp." He moved among them as he spoke. "*Your* task is to keep it in place."

Gabby glanced at her partner, seven-year-old Sabrina, and smiled. "You want to go first, Brina?" she asked.

Sabrina shook her head.

Gabby felt her stomach clench, just the slightest bit. Sabrina was shy, almost painfully so, but she was smart and by far the most talented student in the class. Unfortunately, Brina got so nervous when Francis or her other classmates came near, that no one besides Gabby knew that.

For whatever reason, Sabrina was comfortable around Gabby.

Probably because Gabby was so consistently terrible.

With a mental shake, she forced herself to focus. One deep breath before she closed her eyes and called on her magic—it was ever ready, a small knot of tangled strands in her mind, the pale brown color that matched her eyes exactly, just like every other Rengalla.

Just like Mason, with his beautiful hazel eyes, the strands of his green and gold and brown magic layered together to mimic the gorgeous irises she'd stared at far too often.

Brina shifted and Gabby blinked again, forced herself to focus *again*.

Mason didn't need to live in her mind every second, even if she hadn't been able to stop thinking about him—

Enough.

Remembering her loss of control during the Post-It explosion earlier in the week, she carefully—*oh so carefully*—pulled forth a slender thread of power. It crawled out of her mind, slid down her spine and arms, and burst from her palms in tiny sparks.

Since she was concentrating on air and not her natural affinity for water, Gabby struggled to only call upon the air around them. It wasn't an entirely simple task—the filtering out of water and dirt particles in order to just corral the atmospheric gases—but she managed.

She was sweating like a pig, but she managed.

But the rules of magic were with her, or at least one of the first directives she'd learned—*like called to like*. So as soon as Gabby managed to filter out the water and dirt and had a pure ball of air formed, other gases were attracted to the small sphere.

Soon enough she had a palm-sized ball of gas.

But this was the part that was tricky. She had to stop the flow of those gases and keep her little globe of air contained. To not let it grow and get out of control.

That was what had gone so wrong a few days before.

During the Post-It incident, her sphere had rapidly sucked in the surrounding gases and because she was a novice, still learning how to turn her powers on and off, it had only taken a heartbeat for her power to spiral out of control. Still, she was getting at the whole control thing, especially with her natural element of water.

Air, not so much.

But she struggled onward and forward.

Someday this would all get easier.

Or at least that was what she kept telling herself.

"All, right," she said as soon as she was able. "I'm ready." At the rate the small bit of magic was zapping her strength, her powers would be depleted in minutes.

"Okay," Brina said. "I'll push your ball."

Gabby nodded and braced herself as the chocolate brown thread of Sabrina's powers slid toward her.

It floated closer.

And closer still.

The moment the Brina's magic made contact with hers, every bit of control Gabby had managed to wrestle disappeared in an instant and she lost hold of the sphere.

Pop!

The ball of her power unraveled with a sudden burst of air, loud enough to freeze everyone in place.

"Sorry," Gabby said, her eyes watering from the abrupt gust. Poor Sabrina's hair looked like it had gotten stuck in a blender, her wild curls even crazier than normal because of Gabby's ineptness.

"That was the *coolest* thing I've ever seen," Robert, a toe-headed five-year-old said from behind them. Awe made his voice pitch across the clearing and every pair of eyes in the large space turned toward them.

Gabby felt her cheeks go pink—hell, they didn't just go pink, rather they turned a shade of rip-roaring, raging, fire engine *red*.

Francis walked over, and it was the first time that she had ever seen irritation in his expression. That was directed at her—

Shit.

"I'm sorry—" she began.

"Come with me." He turned to the class. "Children continue. Sabrina, join Robert's group."

As she followed Francis to the edge of the clearing, Gabby's heart plummeted down to her toes, her legs shook. This was the moment he would find out. This was when she would lose everything.

He stopped.

She steeled herself and mirrored the movement.

Francis' eyes locked onto hers as silence stretched between them, and Gabby found herself unable to look away. She'd always thought that the pale blue, the same color as the summer sky, was beautiful. But directed at her, piercing straight into her soul, all traces of kindness and understanding having withered away—

That was completely different.

After a long moment, she spoke. "I'll go."

A flash of disappointment crossed his face and the sigh that slipped between his lips was a long *hiss*. "I think that's for the best. Until you learn control, you'll need to train with those who can protect themselves if something goes wrong." He grimaced. "When I think about what could have just happened—"

Abruptly everything seemed so much worse. "What could have happened?"

Francis gaze was steady, but she read the truth in his expression.

"I could have hurt someone?" she asked, eyes burning. She could have hurt Sabrina? Sweet, innocent Sabrina? Or Robert? Or Daniel?

Compassion made an appearance on Francis' face. And it made everything so much worse. She didn't want Francis to pity her. She wanted to be like everyone else. But there was empathy in those blue depths, he didn't mince words. "You hit Sabrina in the head, dear. If the impact had been stronger or more direct, it could have caused brain damage."

"Oh God." Bile burned the back of her throat and one hand came up to cover her mouth. She bit down on her tongue hard. It was so much worse than Post-Its or making Sabrina's curls even crazier.

The fact that she could have hurt someone. Just like—

A hand touched her shoulder. It was daylight and the soft rustling of trees, the occasional chirp of a bird surrounded her.

It was vastly different than the events that haunted her memories. But she still jumped. Still, her heart rate still shot into the stratosphere and sweat coated her body.

Francis immediately stepped back. It became easier to breath.

"Forgive me," he said. After a moment he continued, "I know it wasn't intentional, dear, and you must understand that I only have your best interests in mind. I wish you would consider the private lessons—"

"I won't take up any more of your time," she broke in. When it looked as though Francis would protest, she added, "I'll consider the lessons. Really. I will."

His expression went stern and Gabby wondered if he'd so easily seen through her blatant lie. It appeared so.

"You'll—"

"I'll train her."

Mason's voice penetrated the tree line and Gabby had two distinct thoughts—

How long had he been standing there? How much had he seen?

The pitying expression told her enough. He'd seen *everything*.

More shame. So much fucking shame. Five-year-olds could control their magic better than her, were infinitely more skilled. It had been bad to screw up in front of the class. Worse to be singled out by Francis. Worse still that she might have injured that innocent little child.

But even multiplying that shame and humiliation by a thousand wouldn't encapsulate the disgust that filled her in that moment at seeing Mason walk from the trees after having born witness to the multitude of her mistakes—

"Excuse me," she managed to croak out. Then she did what she did best.

She ran.

SIX

Mason

HE WATCHED Gabby's face fall, her cheeks go bright pink, and those pretty brown eyes locked with his for a split second before she whirled away and all but sprinted for the tree line. *Fuck.*

Because that glimpse had showed him enough.

She was hurting.

Fuck, again. Mason had been married to Victoria long enough to know he'd bungled something. Unfortunately, he just didn't know what it was. His gaze flicked to Francis, and he raised a brow.

"Ah. To be so young," Francis said lightly, but there was concern in the professor's eyes.

"I'm not *that* young," Mason replied. "What's wrong with her?" he asked into the silence that fell.

"*That* I'm not so sure of." Francis glanced toward the clearing where the kids were chattering. "Daniel," he called, "keep the sphere smaller." His stare returned to Mason. "She's got a large reservoir of power, but she's too tentative. Too jerky.

It makes her dangerous in the way a new recruit is when first learning how to handle a grenade."

Having spent several hundred years with the man in front of him, Mason understood the seemingly obscure connection. "She pulls the pin too soon and threatens to blow up everything around her?"

"Exactly."

"Damn."

There was a beat of silence before Francis spoke again. "I don't think it's a bad idea for you to teach her. I've wanted to study with her privately for a while now, but she's resistant. Perhaps you can convince her otherwise."

"I don't know why she would listen to me."

"I don't know why she wouldn't," Francis said. "You can be very charming. When you try, that is."

Mason scowled. "I think I should be offended."

Francis' eyes glimmered with amusement. It was a side of the teacher that the others didn't often see. But Mason knew that the older Rengalla had a wicked sense of humor. Though that humor wouldn't be driving him in this mess with Gabby. Francis was compassionate to his marrow, and it was easy enough to see he was concerned.

"I'll help her," Mason promised, the words an unwilling, but necessary responsibility.

Francis had been there, had pulled him from the darkness after Victoria's death at the hands of the Dalshie. He'd do anything for the other man.

Damn. Sometimes he really hated having ties to the people around him.

"Don't wear that martyred expression," Francis told him. "She's a pretty woman who needs your help. Play the rescuer." A nudge of Mason's shoulder. "Live a little. Have some fun."

The cavalier way with which Francis spoke made the old

anger rage, the full force of what he'd lost flooding Mason's mind. It was only the massive amount of respect he held for the older man that stopped Mason from snapping out a retort he would no doubt regret later.

Francis tilted his head, his eyes no longer amused. They'd paled, were lined with sadness, with sympathy that threatened to crack the ice around Mason's heart.

"No fun then," Francis murmured. "Just do your best." He was quiet for a moment. "*You* deserve your best effort."

With that cryptic statement, Francis turned back to the class, leaving Mason struggling for the cool dispassion that had served him so well the last decades.

It several minutes for him to find it.

Then he turned and continued in the same direction as Gabby.

Very little effort was required to track her down. Besides the obvious trail of footprints and broken plants, Mason felt a sort of instinctual draw toward her. In fact, that draw was strong enough that he had the uncomfortable thought that if he'd closed his eyes and focused on Gabby, on her silky blonde hair, her pale brown eyes, on her slightly tart lemon and lavender scent, he could teleport to her in moments.

But he didn't take advantage of that instinct, wasn't willing to tempt fate or admit even to his own brain that there was some sort of connection between them.

Because it was wrong.

Any ounce of attraction to another woman disrespected his wife, blurred the memory of his son. Jacob had only been four years old—

The soft sound of sobs broke through the barbed remembrance slashing across his mind, made his heart throb at the wrenching noise. There was so much pain in those tears, so much more than just a simple failed assignment.

It reminded him again that he didn't know anything about Gabby.

She'd only been at the Colony for half a year, brought here after John had found her on one of his missions to seek out and destroy the Dalshie. Maybe it made him an asshole, but Mason had never bothered with the details before, not with so many of their number retreating to the Rengalla's home base over the last months, but he'd finally read the report the previous evening.

Her father had died, and Gabby had been held captive for several months before managing to contact the Colony.

She was lucky, really.

Sometimes the Rengalla who lived off the grid simply disappeared. Sometimes they had no way to contact the Colony if they got into trouble. And while John and his team did their best to keep track of those who didn't stay at the Colony, there were always a few Rengalla who slipped through the cracks. Especially those like Gabby, whose parents moved so often that the file of their previous addresses was at least ten pages long.

Still, Gabby was one of the fortunate ones. She'd been able to contact John, been able to seek out help from her fellow Rengalla. They weren't a large people, but there was strength in living with one another, in laughing and loving together.

Strong. Lucky. Fortunate.

Somehow he doubted very much that she was feeling any of those things at the moment.

Carefully, he pushed through the bushes dotting the sides of the trail and sat down next to her. She hadn't gone far, had merely slipped between some of the freshly planted underbrush and collapsed.

At his movement, she glanced up.

Her tear-streaked cheeks, her reddened and puffy eyes were a bullet to his gut.

He flinched back, trying to ignore the sharp jab of remorse as her face fell.

"I'm okay," she said, voice hoarse. "Just go about y-your day." With that, she turned away, her hands coming up to cover her cheeks. The sobs were quieter as she rose to her feet, but no less destructive to his resolve. Leaves rustled as she pushed through the brush, her shoulders stiff, her gait unsteady.

"Gabby."

He stood and followed her, witnessed the terse shake of her head.

"Leave me alone." She moved faster, headed for the exit.

Irritation welled through him, because he seriously hated it when people ran from their problems. Why couldn't she just be reasonable and deal with this? Or shove it down, lock it up, and throw away the key like he had?

"Gab—"

"Just go!" she shouted.

"Dammit," he growled, losing the final thread on his temper and teleporting across the distance she'd gained. He grabbed her arm. "Just *stop*."

His tone made her jump, but it was his touch that made her cringe.

Unlike their interaction in the infirmary, he released her immediately.

She stumbled backward then tripped and landed on her butt, horror taking the place of his anger. She'd been through a trauma. She needed understanding, not him growling at her.

"I'm sorry," he said, extending a hand to help her up.

She cringed and he drew back his hand, not wanting to make things worse, not when he'd already bungled them to hell and back. Something very much like regret— no, *guilt*—swelled within him. It was an uncomfortable, unfamiliar feeling, especially when his emotions had been locked down for so many years.

But he found that he couldn't concentrate on the whirlwind in his mind, not when embarrassment and shame was whipping across Gabby's face.

A second later, her expression cleared, becoming placid, all traces of emotion wiped clean.

Like an idiot, his instincts had him reaching for her, almost aching to clasp her hand in his, to tug her against his chest and hold her close. "I'm sorry, sweetheart. I shouldn't have—"

"Don't touch me," she said, her voice somehow both shaky and firm at the same time. "Just . . . leave me alone, Mason."

This time when she left, he let her go.

SEVEN

Gabby

"STUPID," she muttered to herself a little while later as she puttered around the break room in the infirmary, taking random things out of the cupboards and putting them back without using them. "Stupid. Stupid. *Stupid.*"

"That sounds like such an important conversation that I hate to interrupt." Suz's droll voice drifted from behind her, up and over Gabby's shoulder.

She stiffened, hands frozen on an empty coffee cup.

"Aw, sweetie," the doctor said. "I'm just kidding." The taller woman came further into the room, leaning around to meet Gabby's eyes even though she tried to her best to avert them. "What's wrong? Have you been crying?"

It was useless to deny what was obviously the truth, so Gabby settled for an attempt at distraction.

"How's your boyfriend?" she asked.

Suz plunked her hands onto her hips. "You know damn well he's not my boyfriend, and sidetracking me won't work. God woman, you're as bad at it as Dee is. Now, tell me what's the matter."

She wrinkled her nose. "I don't want to talk about it."

"That, at least, is an honest answer," Suz muttered. "And if you don't want to talk about it, we won't. But if it's causing you so much pain that it's clear as day to anyone that you're hurting just by getting a glimpse of your face, or by watching you move . . . hell, it's even laced into every word you speak." She brushed her fingers down Gabby's arm. "Then, sweetheart, you need to find *someone* you can talk to."

She nodded, even knowing that wouldn't happen, even as her mind flitted to the flash of compassion she'd seen in Mason's eyes just before she'd run like a freaking coward. It would be tempting, so tempting to allow someone—okay, to allow *him*—to shoulder her burdens. But she'd spent the last months finally fighting for her life, for the chance to live. *No* one would take that from her.

And yet when it came down to it . . . Gabby still needed to learn how to control her powers.

Oh. *Oh.*

"Can I take the rest of the day off?" she asked abruptly.

Suz blinked, clearly taken aback. Not that Gabby could blame her. She'd taken a sharp left in their conversation, but it was also the first instance she'd asked for time off, and though she felt guilty for even broaching the subject, pieces of a plan were lining up in her mind.

Perhaps there was a way to learn control without endangering anyone else.

Suz's golden brown eyes gentled. "Of course. Why don't you take tomorrow as well?"

Gratitude enveloped Gabby and she impulsively hugged the woman who'd become her closest friend over the last half a year. "Thank you," she whispered.

Suz stiffened and it took a second before that tension faded and Suz hugged her back. It wasn't that Gabby *never* touched anyone. It wasn't even that she didn't enjoy the hugs, the soft pats that were intrinsic to the culture of the Colony. She liked how they made people feel connect, like they were part of a family. It was just that—

Walls slammed down in her mind.

She didn't want to conjure the memories. They were so tangled and twisted up, and she couldn't afford to get sucked down that dark tunnel of affection and pain, terror and love. She didn't want to remember how the beautiful, sweet smile that had always adorned her mother's face become twisted and cold, nor how one day everything changed.

The hand descending, the open palm cracked across her face.

How it had stung so, so much.

That had been the first sign, but, unfortunately, not the last. And after that day, things had deteriorated so rapidly that she hadn't known what to do. She had tried to fix everything. To make it all better.

Of course, that had proved impossible.

The stifling fear of that final night continued to eat at her, threatened to consume her, to transform her into a sniveling pile of worthless tissue.

No. She wouldn't let it. But—

If John hadn't come, she would have—

No. Piece by piece, frame by frame she locked away the memories, the remembered pain and terror.

No more.

With that thought, she realized she was still hugging Suz. Ugh. She was so fucking messed up. Releasing her friend, she said goodbye then left the infirmary, making a pitstop at her favorite locale—the supply closet.

The one she stopped at was fully stocked and she paused only long enough to snag one of the stocked backpacks hanging inside. Then she shouldered the pack, and walked straight out the front door of the Colony. She crossed the front lawn, bypassing the small lake of sparkling navy waters. Her focus was on getting away, moving far from where she might hurt, might do damage, and she wanted . . . something that reminded her of home, of her life before things had so irrevocably changed.

It didn't take long for the peaceful oblivion of the forest surrounding the Colony to swallow her whole.

THE PATH WAS WORN and winding.

Her feet ached.

She'd wanted to get lost in the wilderness, to pretend as though the darkness that had eclipsed her life didn't exist.

Only . . . she'd forgotten about the shield.

To create it, Cody and Daughtry had used Bond Magic—a special form of their powers that only existed when two people were bonded. Somehow the mental and magical connection meant their powers were combined on an integral, soul to soul level.

That magic was stronger.

Stronger than *anything* any other Rengalla could manifest.

Which was why they'd used it to protect the Colony.

But that magic had limits, and in this case, the shield could only be so large before its integrity became compromised.

Much like a bubble that had been blown too big, every time Daughtry and Cody worked to expand the shield to cover more of the surrounding area, it had become unstable.

Large bald patches had appeared randomly in the knitted

threads of emerald and violet that was their Bond Magic. At first, they had tried to repair them, but it had taken too much energy to keep up with the rapidly appearing holes.

Thus, the decision had been made to shrink the shield.

It still encompassed an area in the tens of acres, but between the Colony itself, the various outbuildings, and the wide swathe of cultured gardens surrounding them, there wasn't much wilderness left.

At least not much that she could access.

In the end, Gabby decided that she'd find the quietest, most out of the way corner and come hell or high water, she would find a solution to the problems plaguing her.

It took a good two hours of wandering to find a workable place.

By the time she dropped the pack and sank down onto her butt, resting her aching feet, the sun was high in the sky. Dappled sunshine slanted through the trees to make pretty patterns on the dirt around her, the wind whistled softly through the leaves. The space she'd commandeered was right next to the outer barrier of the shield, meaning the light faintly tinged by the violet and green strands of magic.

Which gave the trees and ground an unearthly feel, but it was just as well, because it wasn't scenery Gabby had been searching for.

She needed privacy.

No one came out this far. Not with the Dalshie's recent attack still so fresh in everyone's memory.

For her purposes, it was perfect.

"Okay," she whispered. "Deep breaths. Relax." Easier said than done, of course, but she forced herself to sit quietly, to focus on the rustles of birds, the squawking protests of squirrels, and eventually she found herself settling in. Sadly, those quiet minutes were the most peaceful moments she'd had in months

—*hell*, in years. In fact, she couldn't remember the last time she'd been able to just sit somewhere and fully let down her guard.

Not since the day of the slap.

Not since she'd noticed the black mark that signified the descent into madness, into dark magic and immorality had first appeared on—

A tree branch snapped.

Her eyes flew up, something inside her already knowing who was closing in.

Irritation engulfed her. He'd already intruded on her thoughts, had witnessed her failures. What more could the man want?

Mason's slightly shaggy brown hair fell into his eyes as he bent under a low-hanging branch, his stare unerringly locking onto hers as he crossed the last few feet between them and stepped into the small clearing she'd claimed as her own little slice of sanctuary.

So much for that.

It hadn't even been thirty minutes before her fragile peace was shattered.

He frowned at what must have been a surly expression on her face. "Not happy to see me, Gabs?"

Annoyance made her reply icy cold. "My name is Gabrielle. Or Gabby. It is *not* Gabs." The latter sounded like an insult, as though she could never hold her tongue, and it reminded her too much of the many times her mother had told her to be shut up.

"Gabby, then," Mason said. "You've been making it a habit to run from me."

"I didn't run," she said, her chin lifting.

He raised a brow.

"I think of it more as a tactical retreat," she said.

He laughed at that, loud and long, even though Gabby hadn't exactly meant for it to be a joke.

To be the source of his amusement didn't sit well with her.

To be slapped in the face with his musical laugh, his smiling face, and his insane body was even worse.

After a minute he spoke. "So tell me then, why the *tactical retreat?*"

Which happened to be both the simplest and the most diffi-cult question anyone had ever asked her.

She nibbled at the corner of her mouth, whispered, "I don't know."

"Well, I'll just sit over here until you figure it out." He made to lean back against a tree.

Irritation in her veins. "You need to go."

Her body wanted him, even though her heart and mind were petrified. And that fear won out over anything else. It had to. Because she'd learned to trust her instincts, to trust the voices inside that had kept her safe.

If they said run, she ran.

If they told her to keep her distance, she built concrete walls.

If—

"You can't stay out here by yourself."

She rolled her eyes, anger turning her tone tart. "I've stayed in places a hell of a lot worse than this."

He tilted his head and she had the distinct and ominous feeling that she'd just given him the opening he'd been looking for.

"Oh yeah?" His question was casual. "Tell me about it."

Shit. Yup. She'd walked right into that one, and not knowing what to do, what to say, she fell silent. Unsurprisingly, the quiet didn't appear to bother him. He sank down next to her, mirroring her movements, resting his back against the tree trunk.

Several minutes of silence later, he said, "I won't tell anyone."

She almost snorted. He would sure as hell tell somebody *something*. If he ever found out, the man who'd lost everything because of—

"Don't do that."

Her eyes flashed up. "Do wh-what?"

His hazel eyes were gentle. "Don't allow the horrors in your mind to make you so sad."

What? How—? She shook her head, steeled her spine. "You don't know what you're talking about."

He sighed, a soft, put-upon sound. "I know much more than you'd think."

"You don't know what happened," she said. "What I've—"

Just barely, she managed to squash the sentiment.

"What you've . . ."

She shook her head, unable to trust that she could confide in him. Her own family had turned against her, why would a man she barely knew be different?

Still, there was a part of her, a swell of emotions just under her sternum that encouraged her to take the risk. But that ball of feelings wasn't big enough—at least not yet.

And so the quiet stretched, becoming more strained by the moment.

He sighed again, and bent his knees, his elbows coming down to rest atop them and she couldn't stop from staring at him —at his broad chest, his flat abs, the bulge of his biceps below the cuffs of his t-shirt—

"No one will judge you here."

A snort escaped her.

"This isn't a utopia," she said. "People judge. *Everywhere*. And I'm far from innocent."

EIGHT

Mason

HE HAD no idea what to say, not with Gabby's miserable light brown eyes miserable on him, the invisible weight of her memories physically slumping her shoulders, flattening out the lush lines of her mouth.

His Victoria had been nothing like the woman in front of him. If he'd demanded answers, Victoria would have provided them.

Gabby was a modern woman—which was fine, except he didn't know how to negotiate with modern women. It had been a hundred years since he'd even noticed a member of the opposite sex beyond the cursory inspections that men conducted on every female they saw.

And there was nothing cursory about Gabby. Not the way she looked, not the way he felt about her.

His heart beat a little faster in her presence and blood pooled in places he'd thought long desensitized.

It wasn't that he'd been immune to women since his wife

died. He appreciated the opposite sex—though in the way that someone who knew nothing about wine could simply enjoy the flavor of it.

There was no passion, no rapid pulses, or inconvenient blood flow.

Those other women had been nothing more than a passing curiosity. A vague appreciation because he wouldn't disrespect Victoria's memory by allowing it to be more. But with Gabby, it wasn't a matter of tempering his curiosity, of that vague appreciation. His mind was fascinated. His body drawn to hers in a way he couldn't ignore. And his powers—

No.

He shouldn't be here.

He wasn't illogical enough to think that Victoria wouldn't have wanted him to move on with his life, but this fascination with Gabby—the curiosity bordering on obsession he'd tried and failed to wall off and ignore, the attraction, the way his powers stood up and took notice when he was with her—was completely different.

It wasn't just moving on. It threatened to decimate his past.

To undo everything he'd spent decades clinging to.

"You can go." Her voice was quiet, yet laced with steel.

And he finally admitted the truth, both aloud and inside his heart. "I *can't*." Despite the turmoil inside him telling to run, and regardless of the insidious piece of his soul that wanted him to stay, the one that was so much stronger than his urge to flee, he'd *promised*.

She leaned back against the tree, sighed. "Why?"

"I told Francis—"

Mason realized his mistake immediately and snapped his mouth closed, shutting off the flow of stupidity. Rusty. His instincts were rusty.

The moment that he'd mentioned Francis, Gabby's face had fallen.

Her recovery was quick, though, impressively so. Light brown eyes iced over and her chin came up.

"Leave," she snapped, pointing toward the Colony.

For some reason, the order irritated him.

So instead of abiding it, he made a show of leaning back against the tree, of stretching his legs out in front of him. "No can do, Sunshine."

Somehow her expression went even colder. "Excuse me?"

"Since I'm responsible for tutoring you, I think it's best if we begin our first lesson right now."

"And what lesson would that be?" she asked, her teeth clenched, the question gritted out.

"Control."

Something interesting went across her face at that single word.

Hope and fear were chased by such bone-deep longing that he actually *felt* the crack forming in the armor around his heart. And she must have sensed it, or at least seen a sign of it in his expression, because her eyes widened and though she leaned back a fraction, her voice softened.

"I—Do you really think I could—?" Her blonde ponytail bobbed as she shook her head. "Never mind," she said. Her sentences ran together as she rushed on. "I've decided I should take a break from the magic. Wait until I've settled in more. Until I'm more comfortable, until my emotions have steadied and—"

"Why would you think that emotions had a single thing to do with control?"

"I—uh." She paused, head cocking to the side. "They don't?"

"Of course they do," he said. "Just not in the way you're thinking."

Her eyes darkened, and he guessed it was in irritation. Unbidden and unexplainably, a blip of happiness swelled up inside him. He paused, analyzed the emotion, and realized it was because he affected her. She couldn't ignore him, not completely anyway, even if she tried.

He got to her. Maybe as much as she got to him.

"I don't understand," she muttered, shoving her hands through her hair, knocking her ponytail askew.

"Hate that, do you?" he teased.

Lips pressed flat, she snapped. "You're such an arrogant jerk."

He shrugged. "Been called worse."

Her hands clenched, and the tops of her cheeks went a little pink, but when she didn't ask him the question that was obviously eating at her, he remained silent knowing she'd eventually talk.

She was impatient. Which was part of her problem, albeit a small piece. But one that she still needed to fix.

At ease now that he had an insight about the complicated woman sitting a few feet away, he turned his gaze to the surrounding trees, the worn path, the violet-green shield, and waited. Pretended to be completely focused on everything *except* Gabby. She couldn't know that he was aware of her every minute movement, the way she opened and closed her hands on her thighs, how she shifted her spine against the tree trunk as the minutes trailed by.

Irritation poured off her, a palpable fog that surrounded them.

One that Mason refused to disperse.

He didn't understand quite why he needed to push her in this, why he needed to get her to bend—just a little. All he knew was that his gut told him if she didn't make the first entreaty, if she didn't trust him even the slightest bit, then they would never move forward.

So he waited.

And *waited*.

Finally, with a sigh that was loud enough to make scare the birds out of the tree above her, she snapped, "Can you explain it to me?"

He didn't answer for a long moment, waiting until she was ready to explode in irritation. It was a technique Dante often used with new recruits. Froth them up, make them feel something, *anything* . . . because anger was better than fear.

And in this case, her anger directed at him just might keep enough distance between them so that he'd survive this with his walls in place.

"It's impossible to lock down every emotion, and you shouldn't," he said when her lips parted, no doubt to snap at him again. "In a fight for your life your heart will be pumping, adrenaline will course through your veins. Your mind might focus exceptionally well, but you'll never be completely free of emotion. Terror. Rage. Anxiety. They'll all be there." He studied her as he spoke, saw the glimmer of understanding bloom within her eyes.

Her hands unclenched. "So if I can't even control my magic when my emotions are relatively calm, I'll never be able to in a circumstance where I, or someone I'm with, is at risk."

"Exactly," he said. "Your emotions don't get smaller in a situation where you're fighting for your life. They grow exponentially. Until they feel like they're swallowing you whole, choking your lungs, churning the contents of your stomach." He took a breath as he tried to shove back his own memories, to bury the demons that made it hard for *him* to focus. "Do you understand why it's critical that you cope with the lesser feel-ings *now*?"

She nodded. "If I don't, they'll overwhelm me."

The way she spoke, the careful way those words marched out of her mouth, regimented soldiers in precise enunciation, made it clear to him that she'd already experienced a situation like he'd described—one filled with fear, terror, horror.

What had happened?

Except . . . he wasn't a lover or a friend. He was a teacher.

He needed to help her learn how to use her magic. Nothing more.

"Yes," he said and shoved away the myriad of questions that had arisen alongside the deep-seated urge to keep prodding at the prickly barbed exterior that surrounded her. Part of him wanted to know, to understand. The other part wanted to retreat.

But regardless, he'd pushed her far enough.

For now, at least.

Carefully, he pulled on his magic, readying to summon a small pocket of water. It was instinctual, effortless, even though his specialty was air. Like his brothers, he could teleport, could manipulate the air in a thousand different ways. But he knew that Gabby's specialty was water, so he'd start with that.

The trickle of magic curled down his spine and balled in his palms. It was easy to keep the sphere of water in his hands free of outside pollutants, but he knew that it was challenging for new students.

The reason was simple, and one of those fundamental rules of elemental magic.

Like called to like.

If he called upon water, every bit of moisture was attracted to the magic. Droplets of water on leaves, moisture in the air, the wet dirt beneath their feet. Dust and grime, bacteria, microorganisms came along if the power wasn't focused.

It took effort to keep the water in one's palms pure.

Therefore that was where they would start. And stay until the fear that Gabby had entrenched deep inside her faded away.

"I want you to do *exactly* as I do," he said and expanded the sphere.

NINE

Gabby

SHE WATCHED the ball of water grow in Mason's palm.

Brown and green and gold strands crawled over its surface, fine threads that worked in tandem to keep the moisture balled in place. Between the strands, the water glittered in the dappled sunlight, and instinctively, she knew the substance was as pure as any mountain stream.

Sensing him staring at her, she forcibly tore her gaze from the magic in his palms and brought it up to his face.

The glimpse of hardness, the slight derision that had hardened the lines of his jaw and cheekbones just moments before was gone, and though his expression wasn't kind exactly, and he didn't have the same scholarly concern as Francis did, there was *some* compassion on his face. Well, *that* and a whole heck of a lot of challenge.

Beneath both of those things was heat.

But what *kind* of heat? Anger that he had to be there? Frustration because she couldn't complete a simple task? Or something else? Something deeper, bigger, *more?*

Maybe . . . he felt the same draw she did.

Stupid. Mentally knocking that thought right out of her brain, she settled on the heat being anger that Mason had promised Francis he would teach her. She was wholly incapable. Ugh. She shook her head. Enough of these mental Olympics. Gabby needed control and this was her opportunity to learn—

"No?" His question was hard, biting, the tone making her jump.

"Um, what?" she asked, scrambling to understand. "No, *what?*"

The sphere of water evaporated, wisps of magic disappearing off into space. "You won't practice? I asked you to do what I do, and instead you sit there, shaking your head at me."

Her mind finally caught up.

"N-no," she sputtered. His eyes flashed in irritation, and her cheeks went hot. "*No.* I meant—" Her thoughts tangled as the anger on his face invoked a response she couldn't control.

Her heart raced.

Sweat sheened her body.

Her hands shook.

She felt physically sick and had to stifle the urge to run.

His expression went blank and he watched her carefully. No doubt her emotions were as clear as though they'd been written on a billboard. Without warning, a memory flared to life in her mind.

Clear as day, Gabby Love. Soft fingers on her cheek. Her mother's gentle voice. *Your face always says what's in your brain, even when your words don't.*

They'd been making chocolate cake.

She'd been desperate to lick the bowl.

And her mother had let her.

Her heart squeezed. She hadn't thought there were any

happy memories left. Not when her mother had transformed from a good person into a hideous monster in a matter of days. Not when everything for so long had been dark and terrifying and without any bit of happiness.

God, she'd tried so *hard* to save her and . . . it had all been for nothing.

A shuddering breath tore through her and she forced her gaze up, another shaky exhale trailing the first when it collided with the intensity of Mason's eyes. He wouldn't hurt her, she reminded herself. He was a LexTal. Their job was to protect, first and foremost. But that wasn't what was driving the urge to confide in him. No, that yearning had come from somewhere else. Except . . . she wasn't thinking about that right now. In *this* moment, she needed to pull herself together.

It took a few minutes before she was able to keep her tone even. "The no was for me," she said. "For my internal dialogue," she added when his brows drew down and then—figuring what the hell did she have to lose—she admitted, "I was arguing with myself."

His lips curled at the corners and amusement danced in his eyes.

Her breath caught, for an entirely other reason than fear. He was sexy and he smelled incredible, an earthy spicy scent that reminded her of sandalwood.

"Do that often?" he asked lightly.

She made a face. "Doesn't everyone?"

A little of the humor left his face. "Yes."

"We're a pair, aren't we?" she blurted, thinking that while physically she couldn't be more distant from the man, emotionally they were just two people with really fucked up pasts.

Her question brought his head up so fast that she jumped, the movement so jarring, so unexpected that it frightened her.

Then she shook off the feeling and raised her chin. Her

statement had been an attempt at building camaraderie, at dispersing the tension that normally filled the air between them.

Clearly, that hadn't worked.

But she wasn't going to apologize for it.

Eyes cold, he stood in a single controlled movement, his every muscle in careful alignment, in strict order. He'd made rising to his feet look like the most graceful undertaking on the planet while she made file folders explode.

Nothing could have better illustrated the myriad of differences between them.

Mason leaned in, crowding her and his words were a different kind of hurt. A verbal snap. A rubber band meeting bare skin. Sharp and stinging.

"We are *nothing* alike."

That was true. Even if she didn't have the awful memories of her own personal years of terror, she wasn't *like* him. She wasn't graceful or rich, didn't carry herself with inbred confidence. Hell, she'd lived in a trailer, not the opulence of the Colony. So no, she wasn't like Mason. She was Gabrielle Swinson, born to a mother whose soul had been destroyed, a witness to atrocities no child should see. That left a mark, no matter how hard she tried to forget what had happened and focus on the future.

But to have him dismiss her so harshly—

Her rise to her feet was a hell of a lot less graceful than Mason's.

She crossed to him, tilting her head so that she could glare into the frost that had appeared in his expression.

Any trace of softness or compassion was gone.

And so was she.

It took less than thirty seconds to roll up her sleeping bag and shove it into the pack. She shouldered it then glanced back.

"You're right," she told him. "We are nothing alike."

She took three steps forward.

The shield was hard to move through, a viscous barrier that didn't want to let her go.

"Gabby!"

She didn't bother to answer, just kept moving forward. It *was* possible to make it through. Daughtry had told her that the shield was calibrated to let animals come and go.

Small animals, she remembered a few seconds in, pushing and struggling through the viscous and tautly woven purple and emerald strands, could move through much more easily. Larger animals—such as herself—with a bit more difficulty. But much like one of those finger-trap toys, the barrier itself was carefully designed to keep *out* larger animals and Dalshie.

So leaving would be less of an issue than getting back in.

Now was not the time for that particular worry. She was almost through.

The pressure surrounding her on all side abruptly faded and she found herself flying forward, but just as her face would have made contact with the grass and leaves and dirt, something caught her.

Mid-air—the motion so fast even her own eyes had a hard time processing the movement—she was rotated. A pair of strong armswrapped around her tightly.

Instead of dirt and leaves, her face was pressed into a hard, spicy scented chest, her body drawn parallel with the man's beneath her. And it was a definitely *all* man. Hard thighs, narrow hips, flat abs—

Every bit of air flew out of her as they collided with the ground.

When she was finally able to suck in a breath, she got a nose full of Mason's addicting scent. Because who else could it be? And perched atop him, her lungs struggling to steady, she had the inane thought that he smelled like citrus.

A touch of tangy orange. A sprinkling of bitter. Of acid.

That thought brought her back into herself.

Because she'd felt that acid.

Pushing against his chest until he released her, she distanced herself both mentally and physically. Then, without a word, she turned away. She was leaving. But an instant later, his hand caught her shoulder, stalling her attempts to flee.

"Let me go," she gritted.

"No." He held tight.

Wrenching her arm, trying to put some space between them and failing miserably, her words were harsh. "You're an asshole."

He snorted. "Clearly."

Her struggles stalled.

"Let me go," she repeated.

"No," *he* repeated. His phone buzzed and he exerted careful, determined pressure on her shoulder until she was finally rotated to face him.

It was annoying how easily he could manipulate her body.

"Stay," he ordered, making her temper flare all over again as he reached into his pocket and extracted his phone. His other hand stayed on her arm, his fingers too warm, evoking too many sensations that she didn't want to think about.

Gabby couldn't understand the words on the other end of the line and couldn't discern anything aside from Mason's half of the conversation, but after a few seconds, the fingers on her shoulders relaxed.

Gratefully, she stepped back.

He glared at her and followed.

She shook her head, pointed at him, and drew her finger across her throat. If he didn't give her some space, she would be required to take drastic measures.

For some reason, her actions made him smile.

And seriously, but her reaction to that little quirk of his lips was beyond stupid. Her stomach clenched, her cheeks warmed, and her pulse, well that little S.O.B. sprinted like a thoroughbred around a racetrack.

Still, she put one foot in front of the other.

His words trailed her. "No. No disturbance." He shook his head. "Okay, a *slight* disturbance. Suffice to say Gabby and I are outside of the shield. Good news is that we have our live test."

Ignoring him as he talked, she kept walking. Maybe she could lose him in the woods

A harsh chuckle escaped her.

Yeah, right. That would happen. And unicorns regularly painted rainbows. Or maybe it should be tiny jovial fairies painting replicas of the Mona Lisa. Because that was how much confidence she had in her ability to get away from *any* LexTal, least of all one with the skills that Mason had.

Case in point the hot breath that brushed her nape just as she finished that thought.

"What's so funny?"

TEN

Mason

HE WATCHED GABBY WHIRL, her mouth pressed flat, her cheeks flushed, her eyes filled with anger, and had to fight back the surge of primitive possessiveness shot down into the very depths of his soul.

God, she was pretty.

Fuck, but he wanted her.

"Leave. Me. Alone." Fierce words. Intense anger.

Except . . . there was pain in those brown eyes, and it was no longer just the hurts of her past that soiled the pretty bronze color.

He'd wounded her.

He couldn't pretend that what he'd said hadn't hurt her, but her words—her simple description of them as a pair—had sliced him open more effectively than a blade to the abdomen. So much guilt and regret and pain—

Fuck, Victoria, he thought, wishing that so many things were different. *I'm a mess.*

"I *can't* leave," he admitted.

She probably figured he wouldn't leave because he was honorable, because he was a LexTal and they didn't allow innocents to be at risk.

His *real* reasons were a hell of a lot more selfish and a hell of a lot more twisted.

He wanted to be with her. Despite his reservations and that entire truckload of guilt, he liked her, even though he was expressing it like a schoolboy on the playground.

Fuck.

"I'll be fine," she said, still walking, her shoulders stiff but in a fragile way. As though he could blow on her and she'd crumble. "It was a mistake coming here."

He wanted to ask which *here* she was referring to—the Colony as a whole or simply being outside the shield. But she was still speaking and though the words were barely audible, the sadness laced within them eviscerated him . . . and the hostility inside his heart for feeling something for someone who wasn't Victoria.

"I'll never belong," Gabby whispered. She was angled away from him, but not far enough that he couldn't see when brushed at her cheeks, a controlled, surreptitious movement that only hinted at the depth of her hurt.

That was all the motivation he needed. The words burst from him. Anything to stop her hurts, to make her stay, to turn to him instead of away—

God, he was so fucked.

"My wife and son were killed by the Dalshie."

Her feet did that little skitter-slide that people did when they were shocked. Then her stride evened out and she continued walking.

Mason followed.

"I know," she said, stopping when he reached her side, those pale brown eyes filled with sympathy when she rest her hand on his arm briefly. "I'm sorry."

Then she started walking again.

He trailed behind her.

"What do you think you know?" He tried to moderate the question, not wanting to snap at her, to hurt or scare her further. But when he imagined the things that people whispered in the corridors, the pitying looks, it was a challenge.

She glanced back at him, a simple flick of her eyes that were filled with too much perception and cut past all his defenses. Fuck if he didn't feel the reverberation of that look in the very depths of his soul.

"People don't talk about it," she said softly.

"Then how do *you* know?"

She turned fully, her brows pulled down into a frown. "I *think* you're referring to me as an individual, and not intending that as an insult of my parentage or upbringing—"

What in the hell was she talking about?

"—in which case, I'll simply say that I—" Here she faltered, her cheeks heating, the confident tone becoming tinged with embarrassment. "That I was curious about you, so I asked Suz."

She kept her gaze locked onto his, and as he watched her, attempting to decipher what in the fuck all she was saying, her chin came up. It was late afternoon, and the sun was high in the sky, its bright sunbeams breaking through the canopy of trees that surrounded them, gilding her already blonde hair, making it appear to be strands of gold. In an instant, his mind shifted from trying to figure out what she was pissed about to other, more dangerous things—how her pert, little nose had a sprinkling of amber freckles, how her bottom lip was plumper than the top, how the flash of the pink tip of her tongue as she licked the corner of her mouth in nervousness made everything in him stand up and take notice.

"Mason?" she asked.

Mentally shaking himself, he forced his focus onto her as a whole and not each of the minuscule details he'd been obsessing over.

But Gabby as a whole wasn't that much better for his focus.

Because though she was short and her breasts were small, her *ass*—

Shit. His fingers actually tingled with the urge to reach out and find out how the lush curves felt in his hands.

"You were curious about me?" he asked roughly.

Her lids closed, blonde lashes resting against the fragile half-moon of her cheekbones for a long moment. When they opened again, her eyes were tinged with amusement. "That's *all* you took from what I said?"

He really needed to get a grip.

"Um, yes?" Not exactly the witty comeback he'd been hoping for, but his mind was all but shut down, the urge to claim her riding him with sudden fierceness. He wanted to let loose his magic and wrap her in it. He to trace his hands across every inch of her. He wanted—

A woman who wasn't Victoria.

Everything in him froze and he waited . . . for the stabbing pain of guilt, for the sting of betrayal, for the icing over of his heart.

Instead he felt none of that.

Oh, there was guilt and regret and anger, but they weren't all encompassing, they didn't make him want to shut down. In the same way that a paper cut hurts like hell right after it happens then is reduced to a dull throb, the overwhelming emotions that usually surrounded him had been diminished. *Lessoned.*

Agony transformed to dull throb.

"You realize that I'm nothing like you," she said, pulling him from that shocking knowledge and drawing him back into the present.

"Aside from the obvious?" he asked, his stare tracing her head to toe.

She rolled her eyes. "You're going to bring it down to body parts?"

A shrug. "I guess I am."

She muttered something that sounded a lot like "men" before raising her voice. "What I'm trying to say is that I don't blame you for not wanting to spend time tutoring me. I'm not even remotely close to your league."

Now *he* was frowning. "You're not making any sense."

"I know," she said, and it was like someone had placed a two-ton boulder on her shoulders at the admission. "Look, I'll go back with you, okay? It was stupid to run from my problems. I— I know better."

Mason thought about pressing her, but since he ultimately wanted her back and safe behind the shield, instead he just nodded.

She turned back in the direction of the Colony, unerringly orienting herself correctly without even a moment's hesitation. It raised his opinion of her, elevated the underlying respect he already possessed for her, but it wasn't until the glow of the green and violet shield came into focus before he realized that something else had been elevated as well.

His awareness of her. The urge to possess. The way he was drawn to her, despite all the reasons he shouldn't be.

He needn't have followed her so closely through the shield.

He could have tracked her with his eyes closed.

His magic intrinsically knew where hers was. It would unerringly *always* know.

Not because of his skills as a LexTal, but . . . because he

knew her an elemental level, *knew* her in the very fiber of his soul.

Heart thumping, panic shooting through him like bolts of lightning, he struggled to maintain a calm façade.

Because—*fuck*—Gabby was *his*.

ELEVEN

Gabby

SHE HAD ALMOST REACHED the brightly colored shield when a jolt jarred her from head to toe, mind to bone marrow. Part of her thought it might be how an expectant mother felt when her baby moved for the first time. The rest of her was too stunned into stillness to really process what she was feeling.

Awareness—a soul-deep awakening.

It was . . . Mason. *Inside* her.

Slowly, she turned to face him. She didn't have to search for him, didn't need to look. She knew *exactly* where he was.

This. Could. Not. Be. Happening.

The draw—the urge to mix her magic with his, to strengthen their connection, to link their minds on an even deeper level—was simply her imagination. He couldn't possibly be feeling the same thing she was.

But horror flooded through her as she watched realization coat the features of his face—desire, need, hope . . . then his eyes went cold, his lips pressed flat.

No, she thought. *This couldn't be happening.*

For a second, it seemed as though he had heard her—his head tilted to the side, and he seemed to be waiting for something, for her to *do* something.

But she didn't understand.

Okay, that wasn't true. The evidence had added up, the signs were too glaring for her to ignore.

A bond.

Fuck. Fuck!

He prowled toward her.

"Wh-what's the matter?" she asked.

He didn't say anything, just crowded her, not stopping until his chest was mere inches from hers. His stare raised the hairs on the back of her neck, made every cell in her body quiver . . . in awareness, in fear, in desire?

Damn, she didn't know, couldn't begin to process the whirlwind of emotions spinning inside her.

All she understood was that being this close to Mason felt right.

"What is it?" she whispered when he didn't speak.

He held up a palm. Strands crawled from its surface, bunching together into a sphere of green and gold and brown.

Unbidden, her magic rose and swelled within her mind. It begged her for release, for her to allow it to crawl down her spine and burst from her hands to join with Mason's.

To complete the bond. Like Daughtry and Cody.

Privacy is an issue because your thoughts are never only your own again. The memory of her friend's words when discussing the connection she had with the man she loved flared to the front of Gabby's mind, flooded her heart with absolute terror.

Stumbling backward, she tore her gaze from Mason's magic.

She couldn't.

They couldn't. They. Could. Not. Bond. It simply wasn't possible.

"It *is* possible," he said, gleaning the thought from her mind.

And—*fuck*—it was beginning already. He had a window to her soul and she had to slam the shutters, to yank the blackout shades closed.

"What's possible?" she asked, playing stupid even as her chest heaved and her palms were sweaty from a combination of nerves and the painful resistance of keeping her magic locked in place. Why she could do *that* without issue but couldn't make a freaking ball of water was beyond her. But before she could focus too closely on her magical ineptitude, he spoke again.

"It *is* possible."

She stumbled another step backward, shook her head.

God, she'd wanted to escape Mason earlier, had forced her way through the shield in her efforts, but now that the truth of why she kept wanting to run from him was staring her in the face, she felt as though she could burst through a concrete wall.

Except there were no walls, only a shield she wouldn't be able to get back through and open space with nowhere to hide.

"You wouldn't be able to hide from me," he said, cherry-picking more thoughts from her mind. "I'll *always* know where you are."

Suz or Daughtry would have said something snarky to that pushy statement, would have rolled their eyes and accuse him of sounding like a serial killer. But she was hardly able to breathe, let alone be witty.

Instead, she shook her head, a mute denial. A *useless* denial.

He stepped close, the ball of magic still in his hand. "Let your power flow."

So many things flashed through her mind.

The urge to do as he'd ordered. A bone-deep desire to bond with him on the most basic level, to belong somewhere, to have someone love her. But her fear of doing so, of someone discovering her past far outweighed anything else. She couldn't let desire drive her. Not in this case. She didn't belong at the Colony. And—her gut burned with nausea—if Mason had access to her mind, he would discover the truth she'd worked so hard to keep secret.

Because, in the end, it would come down to whether or not she was worthy.

And there was no doubt that she wasn't.

"Let. It. Flow," he ordered.

He was a dog to the bone, but she'd known that already, could see that reinforced from his expression, feel it in the way his emotions practically battered at her skin.

He wouldn't let this go.

Either she let her magic fly free and they completed the final step of bonding—mixing their powers was required in order to do so—*or* she discovered her suspicions were wrong, and nothing would happen when their magic wove together.

That they weren't bonded after all.

It was shocking how sad the thought made her. Which was wrong, so completely sick and wrong, but . . . it was the truth.

A truth she couldn't accept. Because they *couldn't* bond.

She needed an opportunity to flee, a distraction, to get far enough away from this place that Mason would forget she existed. Surely it couldn't be that hard to overlook her presence. God knew, her own mother had done it often enough.

And suddenly, she knew exactly what she needed to do.

How to push him away.

The words that came out of her mouth were a cruel, awful necessity.

"You'd so easily betray your wife?" she spat, hardly recognizing her own voice, disgusted that her fear would drive her to do something so terrible, and yet unable to keep from doing it anyway. "You're so anxious to forget her? To forget your son?"

He visibly recoiled, stumbled away from her, face paling, eyes filled with hurt.

She turned her back on him, trembling, filled with revulsion at her cruelty, but at least she'd succeeded in pushing him away. Because this time when she left, putting distance between herself and the Colony, her backpack slung over one shoulder, her destination the mountains in the background, he let her go.

TWELVE

Mason

HE STOOD FROZEN for about two and a half seconds.

Then he followed her.

His footsteps were silent, his tracking instinctive and effective. Add in the magical draw, the way he could sense Gabby's direction without really thinking and his ability to teleport with nary a thought, and even if she'd been hours ahead of him, he still would have easily caught up to her.

But instead of doing that, he trailed her through the woods and tried to figure out why her?

And for that matter why *him*?

He'd spent decades avoiding woman, drawing back from any sign of interest or attraction, not wanting to forget Victoria or mar her memory, or—

Hell, he'd been terrified to put himself out there.

Truthfully, it hadn't been hard to protect himself. He hadn't experienced one iota of temptation. Until Gabby. He didn't know what it was about her that captivated him so completely.

Why he followed *her* when he wouldn't have bothered with anyone else, especially after what she'd said.

Her words before she'd run again had been harsh, but true.

As much as he hated to admit it, even to himself, he *was* still scared. Of what would happen if he allowed himself to care, if that caring led to something else.

Bonding didn't equate to instant love, but it did tie two Rengallas' magic together, and that connection meant something—it drew them together on a most basic level, erected links that were difficult to break. And if the bond was eventually severed, if he bonded with Gabby but failed to keep her, if they each were unable to nurture and grow the connection, they would both lose their powers.

Cleary, he'd been hasty in his decision to mix their magic.

He understood that now.

But he hadn't exactly been thinking clearly, his mind and body filled with the need to claim and possess, and it had been impossible to resist the urge to push. Fuck, he'd given Cody *so much* shit about chasing after Daughtry, so much crap about not being able to control himself.

And two seconds after he'd clued into the bond, he'd cornered Gabby, demanding she complete their link.

But as he followed after her, reality intruded.

And the old fears crept back in.

He'd loved Victoria, had been utterly eviscerated by her death. That potential would be magnified exponentially with the bond. It was a mental, a magical, a soul-deep connection, and once formed, it allowed one's bondmate into the inner depths of the other's mind. Bonded couples could communicate telepathically, could sense emotions and thoughts, could view memories.

The concept was old, but the reality was new.

Before Daughtry and Cody, there were no other bonded couples at the Colony. Until they'd bonded, the Rengalla had thought the ability was lost forever. Five hundred years had passed without one and then Daughtry had swept into the Colony, bonded with Cody, and saved the lot of them from the Dalshie.

Mason had a boatload of respect for Dee, not just because she'd been courageous or because she'd fought for the Rengalla. No, his respect came from the fact that she'd stood up to him when he was in the wrong.

Anyone who held their ground against someone stronger and a hell of a lot meaner, earned points in his book.

"I know you're there." Gabby's voice made him start. She took a breath, a long, slow breath that elevated her shoulders somewhere in the vicinity of her ears and when she turned, it hissed out of her mouth on her exhale. "Why are you following me?"

Why *was* he? For all intents and purposes, she was trying to get rid of him. He should let her.

But *fuck*. He just . . . couldn't allow that to happen.

Raising a brow, he took a step closer. Her eyes were puffy and slightly reddened from the remnants of tears, but her expression was defiant.

And, God, he loved that.

Victoria had never stood up to him. Not directly, anyway. She hadn't been weak, exactly, but she had been very soft, almost fragile. There was nothing but strength in Gabby—brittle strength, but a steel will forged by trauma, by pain, that called to him.

To soothe. To hold. To help her through.

Not that she would let him.

Gabby wouldn't hand over her problems like Victoria had,

wouldn't stand back and let him take care of everything. She was too independent, too used to doing things on her own. And while Mase had no shortage of respect for people with spines in day-to-day life, he never would have thought to desire such a thing in a relationship. *He* was the one in charge. He made the decisions. He—

Had never expected to *be* in another relationship.

But the fact of the matter was that he wasn't one to deny the truth or stick his head in the sand.

The bond was a gift. It wasn't something to be thrown away just because he was scared.

It was special.

Pieces settled inside him, his path becoming clear. He wouldn't push the bond, wouldn't force them to do something that couldn't be undone, but that didn't mean he was going to allow Gabby to run away without even exploring where the draw between them would lead.

If it worked out—if they were both willing to take the risk—then they could complete the bond.

He took another step toward her, noting her eyes widening, abruptly remembering her fear, her panic when he'd touched her without warning.

And . . . he was crowding her again.

Cool.

Tamping down on the urge to get closer, to eliminate the distance between them, he forced himself to stop, to shift so his back was against a tree and the trail was wide open, not missing that the moment the exit was in full view, she relaxed. He wanted to press her. He wanted to demand answers, to force her to hand him every one of her memories, her fears, so he could take care of them, make them disappear, vanquish her enemies with proverbial steed and sword.

Victoria would have thrown them at him.

Gabby held tight to hers.

So he didn't demand. Instead, he slid down the trunk of the tree and sat on the ground. Then when her gaze rested on his, he opened his palm and called forth some water.

"Ready for your lesson?"

THIRTEEN

Gabby

SHE STARED AT HIM, her mouth hanging open, the tension in her spine turning it into a rigid steel rod.

She'd expected him to make demands of her.

To force her to return to the Colony. To mix their magic and complete their bond. To reveal *every* single one of her secrets. Instead he sat on the dirt, his face placid, and the little sphere of magic hovering above his palm.

God, she wanted him—both physically *and* magically.

But she couldn't risk letting someone in.

Daughtry and Suz were different. They each had their own painful memories, and despite all the time they spent together, they didn't push Gabby to reveal more than she was willing.

In her experience, men were different.

Hell, in her dealings thus far with Mason, he been nothing but arrogant and demanding.

What was different now?

And why did the thought of his pushiness both irritate her and make her heart squeeze? The kindness that was set into the soft lines of his face, in the warm brown and green and gold of his eyes, made her feel both cared for and weak. But she didn't like feeling weak, and she sure as hell didn't deserve to be cherished.

"You going to stand there and admire me all day? Or are we going to get to work?"

His teasing voice drew her out of her thoughts, and she wavered for several long moments, the desire to learn to control her magic warring with the instinctual urge to flee.

But . . . good God hadn't she run long enough?

Didn't she deserve the chance to learn to control the powers ingrained into her every cell?

Yes, she had. And yes, she did.

Leaving the distance between them—giving herself an exit in the event that she needed one—she sank to the ground, cleared her mind, and looked over at the man who had captivated her from the moment she'd first laid eyes on him.

"Tell me what to do."

A grin that made her brain threaten to malfunction before he began issuing instructions that had her brain scrambling to focus again . . . and struggling to keep up.

It was hard. *Way* harder than she anticipated.

The first thing he had her attempt was to simply call forth her magic and then cut it off. The stop-start exercise was something that she'd done with Francis, but had never really mastered. Before, instead of relying on skill to leash her powers —because she struggled to find that off switch—she'd allowed herself to get to the point where she was tired, and at that point it had been easy to halt the flow.

Because by then it had been more of a struggle to keep the magic pouring out of her than to draw it in.

Half of the little cheats Gabby was using, she wasn't even aware of.

"Those cheats are the most dangerous," Mason said when they discovered that she wasn't even drawing power in the right way. She had no finesse, just yanked at her mind and whatever magic came out of her was what came. Sometimes it was a flood. Sometimes it was a trickle, but she never knew and never could predict.

She understood now.

Both not being able to pull a controlled amount of her magic *and* relying on fatigue were dangerous, but the danger increased as she trained. Each class with the children, every time she practiced on her own, the stronger she got, and without the ability to draw the right amount of her powers or to be able to shut them off properly, she was a ticking time bomb.

It surprised her that Francis hadn't noticed what she was doing, that he hadn't warned her.

Not that she'd given him ample opportunity.

She'd done her level best to disappear in class, then had avoided his attempts to tutor her. Which was why—beyond anything else—she was disappointed with herself.

Fuck.

She'd been so worried about keeping her secrets, and—if she were being truly honest—so embarrassed that she couldn't do something the children could that she hadn't reached out with questions. Instead, she'd been determined to do it on her own, using ultimately unreliable and slipshod methods to get the tasks done.

It was like knowing the answer to a few algebra questions and trying to use that to teach herself calculus.

Hopeless.

Though, last she looked she couldn't give someone brain damage with math.

Which gave her the renewed strength to keep drilling herself, to keep practicing the start-stop Mason was teaching her, long after her body was coated with sweat, her mental muscles exhausted.

By the end of their lesson a whole half an hour later—and God, but she really needed to keep working on strengthening her mind—Gabby was exhausted, her legs like rubber.

But she *had* managed to turn her magic on and off several times. The correct way. And she'd successful drawn the correct amount of her powers more times than not.

"Good," Mason said as she cut the magic and collapsed back against the tree. "Rest a bit and then we'll move onto the next thing."

Next thing?

She couldn't imagine that she would be ready to move on to the *next thing* any time soon. Her brain was mush, her powers markedly drained—though she *could* feel her magic regenerating, trickling back into her mind in a steady flow.

Well, at least if she learned nothing else, she'd gained an awareness of her powers—and the ability to shut them off.

Closing her eyes, she lay back on the springy earth. Mason was a good teacher, she realized. And not bad to look at either. Ugh. That was a ridiculous thought, even if it was the truth. Fatigue washing over her, she remained still, even as she heard— no, heard wasn't right the right word. It was more like she sensed him move, knew that he was walking over to her, closer.

And, despite her vulnerable position, he didn't frighten her. Okay, that wasn't entirely true. She found a lot of things about Mason scary, but she didn't think he would physically harm her. The fear was deeper, and told her that while her body might be safe, her heart and mind might not be.

Dee would tell her to forget that and just jump his bones.

Her lips curved.

"What's so funny?"

She opened her eyes and saw he'd stopped several feet away.

As she watched, he sank down next to her—keeping the distance between them—then lay back and mirrored her position. The man wasn't sweating, didn't even look the least bit tired. She on the other hand, felt hot and sticky and gross, and no doubt her hair was a disaster.

More ridiculous thoughts.

Who cared about her hair?

Biting the inside of her cheek to keep from sighing, Gabby admitted that *she* cared. She wanted him to find her attractive, to want her, to feel even just a fraction of desire for her. And she wanted *that* perhaps more than she wanted her precious distance.

It wasn't that she didn't like her appearance or thought she was unattractive. Sure she had insecurities just the same as anyone else, not to mention that Mason was beyond gorgeous and clearly prettier than her, but she tried not to focus on the things she couldn't change. Her appearance—and *his* for that matter—being one of those things. She wasn't ever going be in a lingerie ad, but she did okay. And that was enough.

But . . . in the few peaceful moments of her childhood, she'd dreamed about finding a person who would look at her as Mason was doing now.

"You're beautiful," he murmured.

Closing her eyes, she snorted. Beautiful, not so much. She was fine. It was *all* fine. But beautiful? Not quite.

"You know, I can sense the direction of your thoughts," Mason said, tone fierce. "And I don't like them."

She didn't ask how he knew what she was feeling.

She didn't need to. She could feel him inside her, ferret out the irritation at her own train of thoughts, and beneath that, she could sense that he did think she was attractive. And even though she knew that shouldn't make one bit of difference, she couldn't stop a blip of warmth from sliding through her heart.

Mason thought she was pretty.

She could feel that, the proof crystal clear in his thoughts.

Which meant that the evidence for there being a bond between them was pretty much undeniable.

"I do all right," she said. "And anyway, it shouldn't matter how I look."

See? *That* was what she should be focusing on.

"Seriously, Sunshine." Her lips quirked at the endearment. "And you're right. It doesn't matter what you look like. Though . . ." He trailed off, was quiet for a moment, and when he spoke again, his voice was husky. A slight rasp she felt between her thighs. "With your cheeks flushed like that, and your hair all mussed, you look just like a woman who's been thoroughly ravished—"

Her eyes flew open, met his, mischief in those hazel depths. "Mason!"

He chuckled and a wave of heat washed over her, fueled by *his* attraction. Because she could feel his desire in her mind and it fueled her need, coating her from head to toe, raising goose bumps on her skin, sending flutters through her stomach.

Her eyes caught on his biceps, the way they bulged from below the cuff of his T-shirt, then on the strip of exposed skin just above the waistband of his jeans.

Flat abs, a dark trail of hair leading south. She wanted to—

Gabby had to actually shake herself. The attraction, their mixed desire, the need to go to him almost overwhelming. But—

The secrets.

Her heart clenched, her eyes swinging away from his to focus on the trees. Because nothing between them had changed. Not really. Sure they'd managed to work together for a half hour, but all of the reasons to keep separate still existed. Her past. Her mother. Her bone-deep fear of trusting *anyone*—let alone someone who could delve into her mind, draw out every hidden memory.

And the truth was that no one would love her if they knew the truth.

Then there was his wife, his lost son.

How could he move on from something like that? How could she even compare?

The soft brush of fingertips on her cheek made her gasp and her eyes flew down to see Mason had come over to sit directly next to her. She hadn't sensed him move, hadn't heard a single rustle of fabric or the crunch of a leaf, and he was right there. Big and overwhelming and . . . scary.

"You're a ninja," she said, trying desperately for a joke because the look on his face was determined and that didn't bode well for her resistance. "You know that, right?"

He didn't laugh but one brow came up, and maybe she was kidding herself, but she thought his expression might have softened the tiniest bit. She tried to focus on his emotions coming across their fragile connection, the gossamer strands linking them together, but her own were too intense. They overwhelmed anything she was getting from him.

Everything he invoked in her was larger than life. The heat, the fear, her magic's urge to rush forth and envelope them both.

He was the rope attached to a ship's anchor.

But her emotions, the secrets inside her, threatened to pull her to the bottom of the ocean. Their connection made her want to let go of that heavy weight, to allow it to drop unhindered to the seabed, to allow the bindings to wrap around her and keep herself.

And God how she wanted *that*—to forget her reservations, to put aside the purposeful distance she kept between herself and the rest of the world, and just go for it.

Just to see what would happen.

Because surely it would be something really, *really*, good.

Except . . . that didn't happen in real life. Good things didn't happen in *her* life.

"What's the matter, Sunshine?" he asked. "Why are you so upset?"

She could visualize a boulder already been pushed from the top of a cliff, the heavy stone pounding down the hillside, toppling end over end as it hurtled for its inevitable destination.

And no matter how much she tried to convince herself that she wasn't the damn rock, or worse, the earth at the bottom that was about to get crushed, she didn't buy it.

One part of her—no doubt the sane portion—was filled with dread, with fear, and fought against the piece wanted to trust Mason, to trust that he wouldn't hurt her, that he wouldn't leave her, that he would maybe, someday, even *love* her.

Which was clearly impossible, she understood that.

He wouldn't be paying her the least bit of attention if not for the bond's influence. Daughtry had made that clear to her. The bond was a magical construct, two powers that were a good fit, regardless of the people who possessed them. It was biology's way of ensuring that future lines of Rengalla would be powerful, nothing to do with Mason wanting her as a man wanted a woman.

The desire was a byproduct of that—their powers' way of forcing them close. It had drawn Dee and Cody together, just as it was pushing Mason and Gabby at one another.

Not real. Not real. Not. Real.

Right.

Now, she thought, mentally nodding, she just needed him to leave so she could strengthen her barriers against him

"You know," she blurted, grasping at straws, trying desperately to change the subject, trying to scour her mind with a way to put him off. But not hurt him. She didn't want to hurt him again. She didn't think she could bear that. "We're probably not even bonded."

He stared at her, his hazel eyes penetrating straight through the layer of crap she was trying to slop on.

"We're *not* bonded," he said. "Not yet, anyway."

"That's not what I mean," she said, knowing he was referring to them taking the final step of bonding by mixing their magic. "I just—" A sharp shake of her head. "This connection between our minds might be nothing."

His lips pressed flat. After a moment, he said, "*Nothing* as in I can sense your emotions? *Nothing* in that I can track you through these woods without a second thought—"

"You could do that anyway."

"I didn't take you for stupid," he said, cutting off her gasp of outrage at being called stupid with a wave of his hand. "So that must mean you don't want to bond with me." He propped his head up on his arm, the couple of feet of distance between them seeming vast all of a sudden, especially when she felt his mind retreat slightly.

Shit.

Because this wasn't about him. He was . . . well, he seemed quite wonderful and she didn't want him to think there was something wrong with him, not when she knew how much that hurt. Instead, she wanted him to know it was about her.

But before she could puzzle out what to say, he asked, "Why don't you want to bond with me? You don't think I'm attractive?"

Mortification stained her cheeks. "No! It's not that! You're sexy and I've dreamed about kissing—" She froze, clamped a hand over her mouth.

Mason slid close, pulled it off, and then laced his fingers with hers. The contact settled something within her, even as it sent a shiver of pleasure down her spine. "So, not that then," he said softly then slipped a little closer, his voice dropping to a whisper. "Also, for the record, I dreamed about kissing you." His thumb drew light circles on her palm, making her nerves prickle. "And I think you're sexy."

"But—" She shook her head. "Your wife—"

Gabby ground her teeth together, hating the flash of pain on his face, hating that *she'd* hurt him. "I'm sorry," she whispered. "I shouldn't have . . ." She trailed off, not knowing what to say.

His thumb had stopped moving on her skin when she brought up his wife, but after a moment, if began tracing those little circles again. "I loved Victoria," he said, pain his words, but no anger. "And we were happy together, but I don't think she would begrudge me a chance at this."

Gabby sighed, pulled back. "But I don't even know what *this* is!"

"Don't you?" he asked. "After five hundred years without a bond, Daughtry and Cody broke the cycle. Now it seems as though we might continue the trend. Is that what scares you?"

"No." She shook her head. "*Yes*. I mean, I don't care that we'd be the second couple bonded in five hundred years. I just worry . . . I might mess something up," she added, floundering for a reason, for another truth besides the fact that her past made her terrified of moving forward.

"No, I don't think you'll mess something up," he said, taking her hand again. "I know you will. I know *I* will," he added when she winced. "That's how relationships work. People do their best, but sometimes—"

He broke off and she nearly gasped as the wave of pain bombarded her mind.

But it wasn't *her* pain. No, it was—

Her gaze flicked up, took in the shadows of agony and sadness within Mason's hazel eyes. Which was when reality slammed into her with the impact of a locomotive. The fear, the past, *none* of it was as important as the man in front of her.

Because not *everything* was about her.

Because he was a person with a heart, not just memories and fears.

And because . . . he was hurting too.

In that moment, seeing those hazel eyes clouded with pain, she wanted nothing more than to relieve his suffering, to regain that little twitch of his lips, the amusement in his expression.

Her heart stuttered, hope gathering inside like so much helium.

And *still* it was diving headfirst into a river of piranhas. Terrifying, anticipating an agony that was sure to come.

She leaped anyway.

Closing the distance between them, she slanted her mouth against his.

FOURTEEN

Mason

HE LAY FROZEN for one long moment before his body surged into action. One hand came up to cup her face, the other slid down her side to grasp her hip.

He wanted—fuck, how he *wanted*—to cup her ass, but he thought that might be too much, too soon. She might have initiated the kiss, but she hadn't given him permission to grope her like an animal.

And despite reigning himself in, despite grabbing tightly to his control, the kiss was still every. Her taste—slightly tart and floral like one of those expensive gourmet cupcakes. The soft curves under his palms, the quiet moan in the back of her throat, the sweetly innocent way her lips moved on his. So yeah, it took every bit of his control to lie back and allow her to set the pace, especially as his body urged—no, *demanded*—that he take, that he strip her naked and tuck her beneath him, that he coat her from hair to toes in a fine sheet of his magic. Still, he forced himself to let her take the lead, managed to reign himself in.

Her tongue touched the seam of his closed lips and gave one long, slow lick.

That was the end for him.

Opening, he slid his tongue into her mouth, delving deeper as he reached down to cup the firm globes of her ass and pull her flush against him.

Sweet Christ, it was even better than he'd imagined.

He broke away, his lungs burning from lack of oxygen, his cock harder than it had ever been. "You taste so fucking good." He pressed a row of kisses along her cheek, down the smooth column of her neck. Her hips bucked, and he found she'd shifted, was straddling his thigh, the heat of her pussy through both of their jean driving him insane—

He wanted to flick open the button, to slide his hand inside—

"Fuck," he murmured and pulled back.

Gabby froze. "I'm—"

"If you're about to apologize for kissing me, don't. Please don't."

"It's—"

He cupped her nape, tilted her head until he was able to look into her pale brown eyes. "Don't," he said softly.

She stared at him for a long moment, her eyes and mind awash with too many emotions for him to process. Arousal was a given, but there was also a tangle of pain and fear and guilt that cut at him.

"Don't," he said again. "I don't *want* to stop. But I promised myself I would go slow with you, that we'd learn about each other before we did *any* of this. That I—"

She released one long slow breath as amusement crept into her expression and the scalding wave of her emotions receded. "Seems to me that it's probably a little late for that, don't you think?"

A chuckle escaped him. "Are you referring to the potential for a life-altering bond?"

"Possibly." Her lips twitched as she flopped onto her back next to him.

He followed her gaze up into the canopy of the trees, watched as the leaves swayed in the light breeze.

The air was crisp and cool, but not cold exactly. Or at least not cold when he was so close to her. And anyway, his eyes couldn't stay focused on the scenery, not when she lay so close. Not when she was an intricate puzzle that his mind was desperate to solve.

"Where did you grow up?" he asked.

Slam. He felt a concrete wall crash down between them, the impact from the heavy barrier making his ears ring. The pleasant expression that had filled her face after their kiss faded. In its place was the careful, cautious mask he was damned tired of seeing.

"Come on, baby. Tell me *something.*" She jumped at his impatient tone and he bit back a sigh. Fuck, he was an asshole. Moderating his tone, trying fiercely to keep it quiet and calm, he continued, "It's not a hard question, Sunshine."

She shifted, just the slightest bit, and he thought that she might run again. But just as he watched the emotions rise to a crescendo within her mind—making their thin as spider's silk connection throb from the intensity—everything faded to cool, bleak calm.

And just as abruptly, he felt guilty for pushing.

Did he want to know what had devastated this strong, capable, complex woman?

Part of him did.

The other piece, the coward inside who was afraid of getting attached and then hurt, of loving and losing again wanted to pretend that she had no secrets. Or that the secrets she *did* have wouldn't impact him in any way. Unfortunately, he had about fifteen too many decades to believe that could be remotely close to the truth. Her arm brushed his and despite the anxiety churning within his gut, his body paid way too much attention to the slight, incidental contact. "Is it really that bad?"

She laughed, a rough and broken sound. "Yeah," she said. "It's *that* bad."

"Sweetheart—"

"Oh no!" She put one hand up in a gesture of surrender. "Don't start with the *sweet* endearments, I can't handle that. Not if I'm going to get this out."

What had been a sinking feeling seconds before was now a full-blown wormhole of dread. But regardless of his desire to run the other way, Mason sucked it up. He was a LexTal. He didn't shy away from tough circumstances or unbeatable odds—

"I killed my own mother."

He literally felt every drop of blood drain from his face. As it flew south, it made a rushing noise behind his ears. He shook his head, sure he was missing something, certain that there was more to the story. "I—"

"No," she whispered. "I did that. I killed her."

He saw each of the following moments in crystal clarity.

The sheen of tears in her eyes.

Her rapid pulse pounding visibly at the base of her neck.

The calmness of her face even as her emotions threatened to shred his skin.

"There was no excuse," she said, her voice steady. "I stabbed my mother in the back when she wasn't looking."

FIFTEEN

Gabby

SHE DIDN'T TAKE the shock on Mason's face personally.

The only other person who'd heard part of the story was Dante—though she knew Suz and Daughtry had guessed there were more to the bare details she'd given them.

Of course, when Gabby had explained to Dante what happened, his face hadn't paled quite so visibly, but the Rengallan leader's gray eyes *had* widened and there had been a certain   I'm-not-entirely-sure-you're-not-a-homicidal-maniac vibe in her interactions with him. She suspected the only reason Dante had let her stay at the Colony after John had come for her was because he knew there was more to her story.

She wasn't being purposefully obstinate or trying to hide the truth.

She just . . . didn't want to think about what had happened.

Because it was her fault. *She* was the reason her mother had become a—

"Dalshie?" he said the word with such disdain that she flinched back. "Your mother was a Dalshie?"

Her breath caught. Her heart thudded.

Was their fledging connection already strong enough that he was able to catch errant thoughts? Terrifying. That notion was absolutely terrifying.

Especially when his face hardened, when his eyes flicked down, presumably to her right hand, which sat open in her lap. Her outspread fingers revealed a palm that was free of the black stain that marked every one of the dark magic users. She wasn't a Dalshie, but understood why he'd looked there. The moment a Rengalla gave into the draw of the dark magic, they seemed to rot from the inside out, all of their good disappearing, and the first sign of that happen was a black mark appearing on one's palm.

"That was why you killed her?" he asked. "Because she was a Dalshie?"

The question was filled with relief, as if it were easy for him to accept that she'd murdered her own mother, just because Eileen had been Dalshie.

There was no judgment in the act, no condemnation.

And somehow, despite everything, that was what made the truth fly from between her lips.

"My mother wasn't evil."

Mason levered his elbows beneath him and studied her. There was confusion marring his hazel eyes, wariness in his expression.

"She was Dalshie," he said.

There it was. The undeniable truth.

"She wasn't evil." Gabby shook her head. "Or at least she wasn't all of the time."

For some reason that made a long slow breath hiss out of his mouth, his relief a heavy blanket in the air. A stifling one because it meant that he didn't understand, that he couldn't begin to understand.

"She wasn't evil!" The words burst out of her and rang through the clearing. "She *wasn't*."

There was a long moment of silence.

He sat up and reached for her.

She flinched back.

He let out another breath and reached for her again. It was a slower movement, but one that was filled with determination. His fingers grasped her shoulders and with one quick tug, he'd pulled her into his lap. A second later, his arms were around her and she had a face-full of the spicy, sandalwood scent that was Mason.

The soft stroke of his hand through her hair, the steady beat of his heart against her ear was all it took for the words to pour out of her.

"Evil doesn't bake cakes for birthdays. Evil doesn't teach her daughter to braid hair and put on makeup. Evil doesn't have the sex talk. Evil doesn't—" She broke off and sucked in a breath, released it slowly. "My mother wasn't all bad."

Which was the problem.

A blip of understanding radiated into the space around her even as she could sense—in the stiffness of his body, the tension in those thin tendrils that had begun to connect their minds— that he wanted to deny everything she was saying.

Their connection was growing, would continue to grow as they spent more time together. First, it would be like this—a glimpse of his emotions. Next would be thoughts and—

Her gut clenched.

"Easy now," he murmured, fingers weaving through her hair, soft strokes that matched his gentle tone.

Snick.

The touch, the words, they penetrated the barriers around her heart, easily passed through the walls she'd erected, like a bullet shattering through glass.

"Mothers don't add fuel to their daughter's fears, don't allow their flesh and blood to be abused," he said. "Mothers do not make it so that whenever someone gets within five feet of their child they cringe back in horror." He tilted her chin up so that she met his eyes. "Sunshine, if she was Dalshie, she *couldn't* have loved you."

Gabby wanted to deny the statement, to yell that he was wrong—so damned wrong.

It was her memories that betrayed her.

Because for every bit of goodness, there were ten moments of darkness. Of torture. Of agony.

She remembered black-stained palms flying toward her face. How the sharp *crack* sounded when it met her cheek, the burning pain that followed. How she'd been hit other places, too, and how much those hidden bruises had hurt. Then there were the insults and the strange men that had leered at her, had cornered her in the small trailer, had *touched* her. All while her mother had stood by, and how her mother had actually laughed when Gabby had begged for help.

Eventually, she had gotten smart enough to not allow herself to be cornered, but that didn't mean the damage hadn't already been done.

Horror.

Terror.

She was broken, a house with a cracked foundation, with splintering rafters and uneven walls. One good thunderstorm and she'd be reduced to a pile of broken two-by-fours and soggy sheetrock. One good shove and she would splinter forever.

But . . . she kept fighting.

Right now, the urge to get pushing through, to forget the past, to find something *better* was strong enough that she wasn't giving up.

"I know you're right," she told Mason, meeting his eyes,

even though shame and regret sat heavy on her soul, and perhaps she didn't like the broken sound of her voice, but that didn't mean she would deny the truth, didn't mean she'd cave in.

Not yet, anyway.

His hazel eyes locked onto hers, the specks of gold glinting in the dappled sunshine. "I know you do."

"But . . ." She stopped because, what could she say?

That she was happy to have let the abuse happen just because her mother had been her flesh and blood? That she was weak? A coward who'd decided that she would rather protect herself than live in the present? That—

"Part of you loves her still," he said, the statement without an ounce of condemnation. In fact, his mind was full of curiosity instead of disgust, as she would have expected. "It not always easy to stop loving people, even when we want to."

Her lips parted, breath flying out. "I-uh—"

That encapsulated it perfectly, and Gabby shook her head, trying to digest the fact that one of her biggest secrets had just been ousted and her entire world hadn't collapsed. All the while Mason looked at her with compassion and empathy and not anger or hatred or contempt.

"It's normal," he said.

"It's not! It's—" She broke off, biting the inside of her cheek.

Because it was sick. Disgusting. *Wrong*.

All of those things and so many more at the same time. Her love for the person who'd birthed her had been morphed into something that was both disturbing and destructive. How could she love a monster? How could she *still* love a monster, even after everything had happened?

That emotion had paralyzed her, handcuffed her in life. Prevented her from trusting anyone with the truth, from having meaningful relationships, from—

"Normal," he said again, still lightly running his fingers through her hair. "You're normal, Sunshine."

She leaned her forehead against his shoulder, felt the gentle weight of his hands shift her upper arms, the boulder that had been planted on her chest finally pushed off her. "You think?" she asked into his shirt.

"I *know*."

She bit her lip. "Really?"

The question made amusement filter along their connection, but outside of her brain he just snorted, his fingers tightening slightly on her biceps. "*Really*, really."

More relief flowing through her. "Mason?"

"Yeah, Sunshine?"

It was amazing how much she could sense. His concern for her, his pity, the tension that entered his mind at another one of her questions. But . . . for all intents and purposes, the elephant that had been sitting on her chest for so long had just been released back into the wild.

She could breathe again.

Really *breathe* for the first time in years.

"Thank you," she whispered and wrapped her arms around him.

SIXTEEN

Mason

EVERY CELL in his head was filled with lightning.

From a simple embrace.

A hug shouldn't be soul-shattering, but it touched him in ways he never would have expected, even as her hair tickled his cheek, her lavender and lemon scent teased at his nostrils, gratitude flowing from her mind to his.

"No thanks required, Sunshine," he whispered, reaching around her to massage the nape of her neck.

Her breath caught, but she didn't shy away, and they sat like that for a few minutes, wrapped in each other's bodies, the connection between their minds growing stronger with each passing moment.

Eventually she pulled back, and though it went against his every instinct, he let her go, and when she didn't run as he half expected, instead she resumed her previous position, flat on her back, her arms behind her head, Mason couldn't deny that it felt right to have her near.

And that right drew with every minute that passed.

That . . . along with his desire.

Because the position she'd taken up had raised her breasts, plumping them, making his fingers itch with the need to cup and hold and stroke. He *wanted* this woman, wanted her so badly he actually ached with the intensity of that desire. It wasn't like he'd remained completely celibate since Victoria was killed, but he'd been careful to choose women who were in the same mental state as him.

Scratching an itch, mutual satisfaction, or even just friends seeking a pleasurable interlude.

Physical with minimal emotional connection so neither of them would be hurt.

But . . . Gabby was different. Already, the depth of his feelings for her, the utter longing in every cell of his body, was so much more than what he'd had with those other women.

If he was completely honest with himself, it even eclipsed what he'd had with his late wife.

At the thought, he held his breath abd waited for the bolt of guilt, for the urge to destroy the fragile threads of what was developing between him and Gabby, but . . . it didn't come, and after a long moment, he stretched out next to her, soaking up the utter rightness of the moment.

"Mason?" she asked again, tentativeness in her mind and her voice.

"Yes?"

"What were they like?"

He turned his head, took in the tautness of her jaw and stiff set of her shoulders. There was no confusion whom the *they* she was referring to, but his dead wife and son weren't topics of conversation that he ever allowed to be discussed. The urge to change the subject was almost undeniable, but the woman lying next to him, soft and sweet, and *scared* that the question she'd just asked would make him explode—but who'd asked *despite* that fear—made him want to bare his soul.

Even though he never talked about it.

Even though the only ones who knew the circumstances of what had happened were limited to his brothers and the older members of the LexTals.

They were the ones who'd picked up the pieces, who'd stopped him from going after the Dalshie without a plan or clear head.

Who'd prevented him from stupidly chasing after an enemy that far out-gunned them.

They were the ones who'd eventually joined him on his quest for retribution.

The LexTals had been born that day. Not in a quest for vengeance, but for justice. For honor and humility. Born in adversity, as they sought retribution. Those words had become their driving force, their motto. The only thing that he'd cared about—

Until he'd met Gabby.

Now the only thing he wanted more than to eradicate the Dalshie from the planet was for Gabby to allow his magic to mix with hers, to link them together. To go caveman and claim her for his own.

But it was more than that, more than just a visceral, instinctive claiming.

He wanted to be the one to remove the shadows of hurt and fear from her eyes. He wanted to make her smile again.

The bone deep desire to do so shouldn't surprise him.

He knew what bonding was like, had seen Daughtry and Cody struggle to come to terms with the intense mental and magical connection. Mason just hadn't expected that *he* would want it so much. Gabby had been around for six months and even as he'd pretended to keep his distance, he knew it was just that—pretending. Because in reality, he'd found every damn excuse possible to go into the infirmary. Close to her, but not. Safe, but slipping down the slope of obsessive. Hell, he'd convinced himself that the obsession wasn't anything more than his body's need for a female.

He'd ignored the mental component altogether, how his mind felt when he was near—the intimacy despite being strangers, the warmth filling him just by being in her presence, the longing to return to her when he wasn't—and he'd done it with frightening ability.

One would think that after more than two centuries on the planet he would know when he was pulling an ostrich and disregarding the obvious motivation.

Apparently not.

Because until the close proximity, he'd never even considered they might have the potential to bond. Okay, potential wasn't the right word. He and Gabby *would* bond. That fact was practically ingrained into his DNA.

"You don't have to tell me." She rolled to her side, resting her head on her palm. "I don't mean to pry—"

He cut her off with a shake of his head. "It's not that." A pause as he tried to find the right words, ones that would do his family justice. It was almost impossible. Plus, the sky above them was almost dark. If he answered the question they would definitely be making camp outside the shield. He needed to call Dante and—

He was avoiding. Again.

Without warning, a memory popped into his head and he felt his lips turn up. "Jacob was precocious." A laugh escaped him. "I remember one time when he couldn't have been more than two, and he snuck out of his room, crept into my study." He met Gabby's eyes, relieved that though her expression was soft, it wasn't pitying. He couldn't have handled pity right then.

"What happened?" she prompted.

"He'd wanted an inkwell earlier that day. Naturally, I'd refused. Two guesses for what he was after?"

Gabby gave a little chuckle. "Was he able to get it?"

"Oh yes." The recollection of the wide swathes of black ink staining the silk wallpaper, Jacob's chubby cheeks, and forehead was directly in the forefront of his mind.

"How bad?" she asked.

"Worse than you're thinking," he replied. "I had to repaper the entire room. Replace the covers on an entire shelf of books. And my favorite leather chair . . . that was unsalvageable and regulated to the dogs."

"*Oh no.*" She giggled then slapped her free hand over her mouth, trying her best to hold in her laughter. But he wanted to see her smile, to see the single dimple that appeared on the left side of her mouth when she grinned.

He reached for her, peeled her hand from her mouth, not realizing how close it would bring them, how quickly his body would respond to that nearness. He had one short glimpse of that dimple before her expression went hot, her pale brown eyes darkening, her lips parting, her breath shuddering out.

"I didn't think it would be like this," she murmured.

"Did think what would be like this?"

Truthfully, he was having a hard time concentrating. Gabby was so damned soft, her skin like silk.

"It's just biology," she said. "What's between us isn't special —" He frowned, and she added, "Dee said the bond is just about creating little magical geniuses. Which means this attraction"— she gestured between the two of them—"is just nature's way of ensuring we get together." He glowered, not sure which statement pissed him off more. That the only thing between them was biology, or that she disregarded the bond because it was based on instinct. When he didn't speak, only stared, her cheeks flushed bright red. "Right?" she asked, perhaps a little desperately.

"You're saying is that this is nature?"

"I—uh—yes?"

He sat up abruptly, went to slow down, to apologize, she didn't flinch back at the sudden movement. Which only served to piss him off more. Because this wasn't just instinct or magic. Maybe that was the catalyst but—

"Only nature?" he asked, knowing it wasn't. He rose to his knees, turned to face her, less than a foot between him and her sprawled form. "That's it."

Tucking her elbows beneath her, she met his gaze. Her chin came up, and her voice got a little stronger. "Yup," she said, the word finishing on a slight *pop* of sound. "Just nature."

A bolt of amusement shot through him, followed in quick succession by arousal. Because her eyes were hot, because he could feel that it wasn't *just* desire. She liked him, and he . . . *liked* her.

"Nothing except biology?" he asked, and slowly, cautiously, his hands grasped her waist, tugged her close. She came willingly, straddling him, her knees on either side of his legs.

"Yes," she murmured, voice husky.

"Hmm." He pulled her closer still, until the hardened buds of her nipples brushed his chest, until the scent of her, the *feel* of her inundated every one of his senses. "There's nothing between us?"

A gasp slipped between her lips when he bent and nipped at the side of her throat. "Nope. Not a th-thing."

More. His body screamed more. Hell, *her* body and mind screamed for more. He could feel the desire in her thoughts, recognize it in her flushed skin, her rapid breaths, the faint muskiness of arousal in her scent. Unable to stop himself, especially as she wove her fingers into his hair and held tight, he trailed kisses along her neck, up her jaw, until finally, *finally*, his mouth aligned with hers.

Embers of desire erupted into a full-blown forest fire.

Her lips parted immediately, and he slipped his tongue into her mouth. She moaned, fingers tightening, nails biting into his scalp, and he held her closer, needing to consume every last drop of her. Thank fuck, but she was right there with him, her lush curves pressed firmly against every inch of him, her lips moving in tandem with his, and in seconds he found himself barreling out of control.

He'd never been so aroused, so hard in his life. His magic had never been so close to escaping his grasp.

The last was what finally gave him caution.

He slowed the kiss, gentled his tongue, softened his mouth against hers.

Because though he wanted her, he wasn't willing to wield their desire as a weapon, wasn't willing to use their tie to push her into something physical *or* magical. And if he loosed his magic, Gabby's would follow suit. He knew it because though he'd just taught her some fledging control, that control was tenuous. He could feel that in his bones, his gut, his heart—just as he'd known that the secrets she'd held close to her own heart weren't as devastating as she seemed to think they were.

God, she'd dragged herself over broken glass for being a child who loved her mother.

How could anyone fault her that?

So he withdrew his mouth from hers and wrapped her tight in his arms, as much to hold her close, to comfort and show how much she'd come to mean in the short months of their acquaintance, as to keep himself from taking more. Then when his heart had slowed, he pressed a kiss to the top of her head, and loosened his grip.

"Let's make camp."

SEVENTEEN

Gabby

SHE FELT her mouth drop open and couldn't do anything to stop it.

"Camp?" she asked, leaning back and looking around, for the first time aware of the fading light and quieting of the forest's noises. She didn't know what she'd been expecting Mason to say after the mind-blowing kiss, but it certainly hadn't been *that*.

His mind should be as much mush as hers.

"Yes," he teased, brushing the backs of his knuckles over her cheek. "You know—a fire, a tent, a place to sleep for the night?"

She glared. "Sarcasm doesn't become you."

One side of his mouth quirked. "Not much does. Now"—he grabbed her hips (and full disclosure, the feel of his hands there made her breath catch) and gently pushed her off him—"let's get to work before it's fully dark."

"Okay." She stood on shaky legs, made her way to her pack, and started pulling items out of her pack. Mason rose up, took a quick look at what she'd brought, then moved off and started gathering firewood.

"Can't you just make the fire?" she asked as he picked his way through the trees surrounding them, gathering up several sticks and smaller logs. "Or teach me how?"

He chuckled. "Of course I could. But sometimes things are easier without magic."

A frown pulled her brows together at that. Her mother had always used magic for everything, from washing dishes to pulling the dirt out of clothes. "I don't understand. If we have the ability, why not use it?"

His head tilted at that, the same small, unconscious gesture that he'd done several times before. It reminded her of a puppy, but she didn't think he would like the comparison.

"Besides the fact that keeping a fire going would be a huge drain on my powers, sometimes I—" He was quiet for a moment, as though choosing his words carefully. "I think that relying on our magic too much makes us less human somehow. Makes us out of touch with reality." He shrugged his shoulders, a dash of embarrassment flashing across their mental connection to collide with her mind.

"But we're not human," she whispered.

He nodded, bringing the load back into the clearing and using the compact shovel in the pack to dig down into the earth. "I know," he said, laying the wood down. "That doesn't really make any sense. We're Rengalla, not human, and we use magic all the time." He shook his head. "It's a stupid thought."

She spread out the sleeping bag. "I . . . it makes sense to me."

His head popped up, his eyes hopeful as they locked with hers. "It does?"

"Yeah," she murmured, nibbling on her bottom lip. It felt weird to casually bring up her mother and the tangled knot of emotions that was her childhood, but Mason knew everything already. "I mean, my mother used it for *everything*. Maybe that's why she—"

Her throat tightened.

Because it occurred to her that she was scrambling for an excuse as to why her mother had turned when others who'd used magic way more often had not.

Suz healed with her magic on a daily basis and *she* hadn't turned. Mason and his brother's teleported regularly. Francis used his powers to teach multiple classes all day every day.

And none of them had turned.

But her mother had. So what was it that made her different or more susceptible or—

Mason's hand on Gabby's shoulder startled her, but not from fear this time. Her body and mind knew and accepted he was there, that he wouldn't hurt her. Rather, this time she'd been simply lost in thought. "I wish I could give you the answer."

Her heart pulsed. This man.

God, she'd been so scared of him.

But inside he was so . . . *much*. "I know," she murmured, taking his hand and squeezing it lightly. "Thank you."

A pause, his hand sliding down her arm, his fingers weaving with hers. "We don't know that it *isn't* the answer."

He didn't reply but she could sense his desire to find a solution for her, to relieve her of her pain. That notion was so foreign to her that it took a long minute for her to accept the sincerity of his feelings. But the evidence was in their growing link, in the fact that every minute spent in his presence strengthened the connection and made it easier for her to discern his thoughts and emotions.

And those thoughts were filled not with the urge to hurt her, but to make her existence easier.

Shock wove through her, made it difficult for her to breathe.

She'd never before experienced the feeling that went along with the expression of being knocked over with a feather. But she understood it now. It wasn't that she hated herself, that she was surprised someone could like her. She worried, yes, that she might turn out to be like her mother, and had certainly battled plenty of instances of feeling unworthy because of how she grew up, of who'd birthed her.

But more than that, she'd never felt . . . special.

God, that sounded ridiculous. She was an adult. She shouldn't need to feel special. Yet one day in Mason's presence, under that piercing hazel gaze, surrounded with feelings of comfort and concern, made her *want* to be special.

At least in his eyes.

Silence stretched between them—not necessarily uncomfortable, but taut with the memories of the past, of hope for the future.

"I'll get more firewood," she finally said.

Her fingers were still laced with his, and at her words, they tightened for a brief moment. The motion brought an irrational bolt of fear through her. *Ugh.* Mentally smacking herself, she tamped down that panic. She'd already established that he wouldn't hurt her, that the connection between them made it so he wouldn't *want* to, but . . . her past was a burden not so easily shed.

Too many men had cornered her. Too many men had touched her.

By the time she'd shoved down her panic, he had already stepped back, already given her several feet of space, and for the first time since she'd escaped her mother, Gabby felt hate—at the emotions that locked her in an impenetrable box of fear, at the debilitating memories that prevented her from living a full life in the present.

She just wanted to be normal.

Because what woman wouldn't want the chance to be with Mason?

He was attractive, sweet, full of genuine concern, and caring. And she was blowing her chance with him.

"I'm sorry," she murmured, her cheeks hot, her eyes darting around the clearing, desperately searching for something to latch onto so that she wouldn't have to look at him, wouldn't have to see the disappointment in his gaze.

But he didn't say anything, didn't move, and when she finally did find the courage to meet his eyes, it wasn't disappointment that she saw.

Instead, it was anger.

And though part of her wanted to recoil, to curl into a ball and wait out the emotion until it receded—as she'd done so many times before—this time she found the strength not to. Instead, she focused, ferreted out the intricacies of the feeling that swept to her consciousness from Mason's mind, and she discovered . . . that he wasn't mad at her. *At all.* The anger mirrored her own, and was directed at the circumstances of her upbringing, the things she'd suffered, the memories that were keeping them apart—

On both their sides.

Her breath caught, and shock made her heart give one heavy *thump* before it settled back down into a normal rhythm.

Because he was mad at himself, too. Because his past, his hurts, his memories were just as heavy.

"I don't want you to be sorry," he said, drifting closer. "Or to apologize for being afraid. I don't want you to apologize for your feelings. You don't owe me or anyone else that. Not. *Ever.*"

She closed the distance between them, clutched at his shoulders. "But I *want* to be strong like you. To move on and move forward."

A chuckle that lacked any trace of amusement escaped him.

"If you think I've done that—" He broke off and shook his head, stepped out of her grip.

Sadness flooded through her, a sharp spike of pain in her heart.

"But you said—"

What? What *exactly* had he said? That he was interested in moving on with her? Pursuing something with her? No. He *hadn't* said that. He just wanted to mix their magic, to bond, to—

They were back to biology.

A wave of pure disappointment coated her like a wet blanket, chilling her to the bone.

He didn't want her. Not like that.

"I—" He stopped and stared at her for a long moment. For the first time, she could actually feel his mind touching hers, brushing lightly, stroking gently. Her eyes burned because it felt so damned right and yet he was telling her that—

"No, Gabby. I don't mean with regards to us. To you." He grimaced when she winced, touching her cheek, voice earnest. "It's *me* that's the weak one. *Me* you should be avoiding. I've had the same fucking nightmare about Victoria and Jacob every night for the last hundred and fifty years. Every *single* night I wake up in a cold sweat, calling for them, wanting to save them when I—I—" He thrust a hand through his hair. "The truth is that I'm not strong at all. In fact, sometimes I think that the past has me in its sharp talons more than anyone else."

No.

It was unfathomable that this man thought himself weak. When she looked at him she didn't see weakness, only strength, only saw someone who was resilient and exceptionally capable.

She laughed, disbelieving.

"You're laughing at me?" His hazel eyes darkened, becoming less gold and more chocolate.

"No," she said quickly and grabbed his shoulders when he would have retreated. "It's just that I—" She bit her lip as she tried to find the right word, the correct explanation. But there wasn't one, so she settled on the truth. "I know it sounds awful to say this aloud, but I guess it just makes me feel relieved that you have something wrong with you as well."

Amusement softened the hard lines of his face, made the pain slip away.

"We're a pair?" he asked, echoing her earlier words.

Her jaw fall open. Then she saw that he was fighting a grin and smacked him across the chest. "You're terrible."

"No," he said. "I'm Mason. And *you're* gathering more firewood."

Rolling her eyes, Gabby turned and headed for the tree line. There were plenty of suitable sticks—small twigs and dried moss for kindling, larger branches to build the fire's strength. She found a group of good-sized logs, but her arms were too full to carry them. In the end, she used her feet to push them into the center of the path, intending to drop the first load off then make another trip for the bigger stuff.

It couldn't have been more than ten minutes before she returned to the clearing but she might as well have been gone for a decade.

Mason had gotten the fire going and erected her tent. He'd even lugged a fallen log close the hole for the campfire. The thought of cuddling in next to him in front of the warm flames appealed to her immensely.

In fact she could almost imagine it, could almost *feel* the dry heat on her cheeks, hear the cracking twigs, smell the smoke.

Until she looked inside the tent and saw only one sleeping bag.

"Um . . . where's your pack?" she asked, suddenly realizing

that him not having one was a detail she *really* should have noticed earlier.

"Inside the shield."

"Inside the—" The sentence petered out.

"Shield," he finished for her, not exactly helpfully. His lips twitched, and he tapped her lightly on the nose. "Don't worry, Sunshine. I'm not expecting to share. You'll sleep in there and I'll stay out here by the fire."

Part of her—certainly a self-destructive part — was disappointed that he wasn't going to push her to share. The rest of her was relieved. She wasn't in any position to be considering sleeping with him, not when she could barely tolerate anyone touching her.

She ignored the little voice in her head pointedly reminding her that she didn't seem to mind most of his touches.

And kisses.

And the way he held her and teased her and—

That wasn't the problem. Yes, she was attracted to him. Yes, she liked kissing and holding him, liked when he did the same back. But it was unexpected contact that was the problem, the stray touches that made her jump like an electrocuted cat. She hoped—no she *would* get over in time, she *had* to believe that.

Shaking off her ever-spinning thoughts, she eyed the ground.

It wasn't the *worst* campsite she'd ever seen, but there were lots of rocks and the entire space was kind of moist. Without a waterproof layer between him and the ground, Mason would be soaked and chilled by the time the sun rose.

"I'll be fine."

She nodded and dumped her pile of sticks next to the pit he'd dug then bent to add several to the fire.

Should she invite him to share the tent?

Mentally, she shook her head, knew she wasn't quite ready for that yet.

He crouched next to her. "You'll just want to—" His voice trailed off and he cocked his head as she added sticks where they needed then neatly stacked the rest. "You've done this before."

"Just a few hundred times," she murmured with a smile, sensing his confusion. "The forest outside our trailer was my escape. The dirt and trees . . . they didn't—" She shrugged "I ran wild a lot." Her eyes met his. "It was actually fun." Of course there were a lot of times where it *wasn't* fun, where terror had gripped her, where she'd hid in the trees praying someone wouldn't find her, whether it be her mother or one of the men—

Cutting the memories off in their tracks, she forced herself to breath.

Her mother was dead, and no one could exact justice from a pile of ash, even if she'd wanted to . . . which she didn't.

Look forward. Move forward.

One step at a time.

She smiled. "Want to tell me how you lit this without making everything around us burst into flame?"

EIGHTEEN

Mason

HE STUDIED HER—THE slight red tint of her cheeks, the way a few wisps of blond hair had curled up around her ears. Just thinking about fire and pale brown sparks had burst to life on the palm of right hand.

Clearly, her power was there, and readily available.

Her challenge was that she was on the higher end of the spectrum of magic and no one had ever taught her to control her powers.

"Did you use your magic often as a child?"

She shook her head, sighed. "No. My mom . . . well, she got really angry if I tried." She hesitated then said, "I think because she'd lost the ability to use elemental magic when she turned, and it made her feel incompetent when I could."

He bit back a curse, wondered again what kind of atrocities this beautiful, wonderful woman had suffered, amazed that empathy and love and kindness had managed to survive in her.

The Dalshie were fickle creatures, jealous and power-hungry, so maybe he didn't understand why one would keep a child, let alone look after her well-enough that she had survived to adulthood. But he couldn't hope to comprehend the way the Dalshie's twisted minds worked, and more important was that Gabby *had* survived. And she was strong, and so damned good inside that the pureness he could feel in her mind threatened to take his breath away. But that goodness also held power. She was strong in both will *and* magic, so odds were that her mother had been very powerful as well.

And he couldn't imagine Gabby's mother having the fact that she could no longer control elemental magic—but her daughter could—thrown in her face made for fun family bonding time.

"What about your father?" he asked.

"What about him?" she asked, letting the magic go and staring at her palm as the sparks blinked out of existence. "He's dead."

He frowned at the way her voice had gone numb. "What happened?" he asked softly, not wanting to push, but knowing that holding on to pain would only make it harder for her to move forward.

"My mother killed him."

A sharp stab of pain lanced through him, the vividness of her thoughts so much clearer than he could have anticipated.

Their connection was growing.

So strong, in fact, that once the initial wave of pain had passed through him, he was able to focus on the garbled images . . .

A hand descended toward Gabby's face. She was little. Fragile.

Mason heard the crack as skin met skin, felt the sharp sting against his own cheek . . .

The images blinked out, faltering along their developing link.

"What happened?" he asked again.

Her eyes clouded. "My dad must have found out that she'd turned. They argued and I got in the way and my mother—" She swallowed hard. "When my dad came to check on me, to make sure I wasn't hurt . . ."

The memory slammed into Mason's mind . . .

Warm hands touched her face, softly probed her scalp, wiped away the blood. He'd told her to get into the other room, had followed her in and locked the door.

"Ouch!" She winced and fresh tears erupted in her eyes. "Daddy? What's wrong with Mom—"

Thunk.

He came out of the memory, found himself on his knees with Gabby crouched next to him, the firewood abandoned. *Thunk.* He knew that ominous sound, similar to that of a pumpkin splitting in two.

"Mason, oh my God," she said. "Are you okay?"

He hauled her against his chest, held her tight. The action was unthinking, instinctual, and didn't take into account Gabby's reluctance to touch at all. He should have waited for her to touch him, instead of grabbing her. Especially after what he'd just seen.

But the truth was that he *had* to hold her. That memory . . . *fuck.* She shouldn't have had to see that, to bear witness to events that were so much worse than he'd imagined.

So he held her, and was just thankful that she let him.

"You saw it too?" she asked tentatively.

He nodded, knowing that he couldn't speak calmly yet. Still, he understood that if he unleashed the rage inside of him, rage at all she'd been through, she would think it was directed at her.

And that was the last thing he wanted.

None of it was her fault. Not. One. Fucking. Thing.

"John came to me when I called," she whispered. One of her

hands wrapped around his shoulder and massaged the back of his neck, trying to relieve his tension even though *she* was the one hurting.

"I know," he murmured, his voice guttural, his emotions still churning. And yet under her touch, he felt them begin to settle. Less tsunami and more giant ocean storm.

"I found the number in a box of my father's belongings. He'd given it to me for safekeeping and somehow my mother missed destroying it when she burned everything else. I think he must have known something was happening." She paused, her fingers tightening for one brief moment before they relaxed again. "I just wish I'd looked at it closer sooner."

He released a long, slow breath. "Was it too painful?"

She rested her forehead against his shoulder, her breath warm against the bare skin of his throat. "Yes," she said. "But if I'd looked at the box closer, if I'd seen the false bottom, found John's number sooner I might have been able to save—"

It was as if someone had grabbed his heart in a flaming fist and squeezed hard.

"Oh, Sunshine, there was nothing—"

"Don't *say* there was nothing I could have done. I should have—" She shook her head. "I could—"

He gently cupped her cheeks and forced her to meet his stare.

"Think," he said. "Don't let the denial rule you. For *one* moment, just honestly think about what you did and try to find a solution that could have magically solved everything." It was part of what kept him up at night, what turned his dreams into nightmares. Because he thought there were things he could have done to save Victoria and Daniel. Pressing his lips to her forehead, he spoke softly. "I think you'll discover that no matter what you tried, the end result would have been the same."

Her eyes slid shut and she didn't speak for a long moment.

But when she finally peeled back her lids, the slightest touch of humor was in those pale brown depths.

"How'd you get so smart?" she asked.

Decades and decades of darkness, he thought, though he merely smiled and pulled her close enough to whisper, "Enough slacking off. Let's teach you how to be a pyromaniac."

GABBY JUST MIGHT KILL HIM.

The fire was blazing, a few pale brown flames that warmed the air around them mixed amongst the naturally occurring orange to blue. She had managed another lesson, had been able to call forth and then reign back it in successfully.

A huge step in the right direction.

More evidence to support his belief that her powers weren't flawed in any way, but rather that her problem had been a lack of knowledge and practice.

So no, it wasn't her magic that threatened to off him.

Especially when she blinked, released a deep breath and the flames of her magic extinguished. She turned and smiled up at him, and Mase froze, desire roaring through him.

And this was why Gabby might kill him.

From blood loss.

Or perhaps blood *movement* was more apt, because he had the perpetual hard on of a thirteen-year-old boy. Every time she smiled, or shifted closer to him on the log, each time her ponytail slide over her shoulder, lavender and lemon wafting up to tease his nostrils, her curvy as hell body pressing against her cotton T-shirt and jeans, more of his blood moved south. It was uncomfortable, embarrassing and—

"You okay?" she asked.

"Huh?" His head shot up. "I'm sorry, I was distracted."

"If you need to check in with someone at the Colony, someone who might be missing you . . ."

Her brows drew together and he felt a blip of—*oh*.

For a moment, he was struck silent by the implication of her statement, by the slight burn of jealousy he sensed in her mind. "You think that I would kiss and touch you if I had someone back in my quarters?"

Cheeks flushing, she floundered for a few seconds before speaking. "It's just that the bond came on kind of suddenly. I'd understand if you had—um—loose ends."

"Bond or no, I *can* control myself." He frowned, irritation warring with satisfaction that she was into him enough to want him for herself. "There isn't anyone else," he said, biting back a smile. "Well . . . except for Jessica, but—"

"Who's Jessica?"

The grin escaped. "Well, actually *both* Jessicas—" He broke off at her expression, at the outrage coating his mind across their link. Laughter made his chest shake and though he tried to get himself under control, he found himself unable to.

"You're not funny," she muttered, but eventually she laughed with him, her eyes sparkling, her lips turned up in the sexiest smile he'd ever seen.

And all at once, his amusement cut off and he found himself fighting the urge to go all jungle cat, to pin her to the ground and take her. This desire to claim her was unlike anything he'd ever experienced before. Part of him understood that it was the biology of their magic that made the attraction so intense.

The rest of him didn't care.

He wanted.

Wanted to take, to loot and pillage her body, to ply her with pleasure until she was too sated to move an inch.

Swallowing hard, he gripped the log he was sitting on, felt the brittle bark give way under his iron grip.

"Mase?" she asked. "What is it?"

Shaking his head, he released a long breath, counted to ten, did every single calming and focusing exercise he'd learned in his two-plus centuries on this planet.

Not one of them helped.

In fact—incongruously—the only thing that pulled him out of the caveman haze was the soft, sweet silk of Gabby's palm stroking his cheek, catching slightly on the stubble growing there. Her skin was cool, a balm to the raging heat that boiled within him.

"What is it?" she asked again.

He reached up and pulled her palm from his face, pressing a kiss into its center. "Can't you feel it?" he murmured, tapping his temple.

"Feel what?" she asked. Tentatively, her mind came into contact with his and he sensed her surprise at the voracity of his desire.

"I'm okay now," he said, trying to reassure her. "I've got it under control." Regardless of how close to the edge he was, Mason would never allow himself to cross that threshold. Never allow himself to frighten her, to take more than she was willing to give.

Hell, he'd teleport himself to Antarctica if that was what it took to keep her safe.

"But *that's* what you're feeling?" Concern filled her tone, and she cautiously touched his arm. "It's so intense. If it would make things better for you, maybe we should just bond—"

He shook his head. "Sunshine, you have to be the sweetest woman on the planet for suggesting that." Smiling when she snorted, he snagged up her fingers and kissed the tips. "But I'm not going to rush this bond between us just because I have the boner to end all boners."

It was more than that and they both knew it.

But nothing had changed. The bond would be permanent.

Once it was invoked, if he and Gabby didn't foster their connection, didn't nourish their relationship, the bond would wither and die. If *that* happened, they would both lose their magic, and would eventually become mortal.

He didn't mind humans, but he didn't want to be one—to be powerless with a short life span. More importantly, he didn't want Gabby to be altered either.

She laughed at his joke, a rich sound that filled him with a completely different type of pleasure. This woman had become so damned important to him, and he wouldn't risk her or her happiness.

So, yeah, he could deal with a hard cock.

"I hear it's worse for the male," she said.

His gaze met hers, no doubt confused since he was so damned focused on his dick.

She stroked his jaw and his eyes slid closed—God, if taking it slow, if dealing with this perpetual need meant that she kept touching him, then he'd move at a snail's pace. Because the contact was ecstasy. It was right—searing straight down to his DNA.

"Are you listening?" she asked.

"Mmmhmm." He nuzzled his cheek into her hand when she stilled. Then smiled as the petting continued. "Male. Worse."

"You're incorrigible." She laughed, but her fingers continued to move over his face then up into his hair. "Daughtry said her book on bonding talked about the biological impact of a bond, and it said the urge to bond is stronger in males—insert something euphemistic about spreading seed and male desires here."

When he snorted, she laughed again but didn't stop massaging his scalp.

A few minutes later, though, her fingers slowed and began

sliding out from his hair. He wanted to reach for her wrists and pull her back to him, to beg her to continue the action. He didn't. He also didn't protest when she returned to her end of the log and picked up one of the granola bars that was their dinner. When she unwrapped it and handed it to him, he ate it.

Thank you, he thought. It wasn't for the compressed, tasteless granola, but for everything else. For being there. For the support and compassion. For touching him as though she cared.

He repeated the sentiment aloud.

Because she was important.

She might very well become the most important person in his universe.

NINETEEN

Gabby

SHE LAY AWAKE, staring through the mesh triangle at the very apex of the tent. It wasn't that cold out and she'd opted to leave the waterproof covering off in favor of seeing the stars.

Or the little of them that she could spot through the tangle of branches overhead.

Still, the fresh air was nice, and she sucked in a large breath of the crisp, pine-scented stuff, enjoyed the way the heavy, moisture-laden atmosphere almost seemed to coat her lungs. It was like being cleaned from the inside out.

The entire day had been like that.

A soft laugh huffed out of her.

Not twelve hours before she'd been running scared, the fact that she'd loved her Dalshie mother eating a hole in her soul, but Mason's reaction made her reconsider so many of her thoughts and actions that she didn't know quite what to think.

When she'd been a child, her father had taken her to one of those traveling circuses, with the pop-up rides and the stands of cotton candy and corn dogs.

She had begged and begged to go on one called Stratosphere and eventually her father had relented.

Quickly, she had gotten way more than she'd anticipated.

Strapped to the side of a rotating room, she'd been spun until her stomach had clenched in displeasure and her throat had burned from holding back bile.

Despite the very different days, the end result was the same.

She was still spinning.

Part of her wondered why she'd been holding on to her fear for so long. Mason understood her motivations and though she wasn't looking for someone to validate her feelings, it was kind of nice to have him agree with them anyway.

But the abrupt change, the weight being lifted from her chest, no longer having to hold onto the truth like a dirty, little secret, had left her reeling. And thinking.

So much thinking, so late into the night.

Eventually, she came to a conclusion.

Enough—enough worrying and obsessing over and punishing herself.

She didn't need to love the Dalshie her mother had become, to accept the cruelty and horrific acts as anything aside from what they were. Awful. Evil. Soul-shattering darkness. But she could still remember the glimmers of kindness, still keep those good times close to her heart.

About a thousand pounds lighter, she turned her focus to Mason.

She could feel him outside.

She'd never wanted someone as much as she wanted him, never even had more than a passing quiver at *any* man.

The parade of boyfriends her mother had managed to collect—dark, unsavory characters who'd as soon take advantage of her as a child or a grown woman—had silenced those urges.

Which was also part of the problem.

Gabby was a virgin.

A twenty-seven-year-old who'd only kissed one man willingly.

The forced embraces of her mother's men didn't count. Because if she wasn't going to feel shame for her mother's sins, then she certainly wasn't going to shoulder those that belonged squarely to those men.

It was funny—odd funny, not ha-ha funny—that she could so easily shed the shame for the sexual abuse she'd endured, that it had never been so voracious or all-encompassing as that associated with her mother.

Perhaps because it had never gone further than a few forced kisses and several gropes of her breasts and bottom.

All awful. All completely and totally unacceptable. But she hadn't been raped, nor even touched beneath her clothes.

Maybe she didn't possess shame because that invisible line in her mind had never been crossed. Perhaps she hadn't been capable of feeling shame because she'd been so damn numb after seeing her mother murder her father right in front of her.

Or maybe it had always seemed black and white because those acts were wrong. Whereas the circumstances with her mother were a tangle of maternal love and hate.

Regardless of all she'd endured, her body was very open to getting to know Mason in ways she'd never experienced before.

But . . . she was clueless.

Okay, not completely clueless. She'd read romance novels and women's magazines in the last six months—loads of them. Heck, she'd seen Cody and Daughtry indulge in very public, non-PG make-out sessions when they'd thought no one was looking.

But she hadn't *done* any of that.

The two kisses from Mason had been incredible. And also more than she'd willingly experienced with any other man.

Her lips curved with rueful amusement. The first man that she was interested in and he had more than two hundred years of experience under his belt.

She didn't know if she should be horrified or glad.

The memory of stubble on his cheeks beneath her fingers, the way he'd held her tight against his broad chest, the sleek darts of his tongue . . . they combined to have desire coursing through her. He smelled like a man, was strong and muscular and so much harder than her. *Everywhere.*

She would have thought after all the times being cornered, after all the times she'd had to fight her way free from unwanted caresses, that she would never be comfortable with someone stronger than herself.

The bond changed that.

Even though it wasn't fully formed, it still foreshadowed enough of Mason's feelings and intentions that she never doubted him. He touched her because he liked her, because it made them both feel good . . . because he wanted her.

And though his need surged inside him—was strong enough sometimes that when combined with her own desires, it seemed as though it would scorch *her* from the inside out—he didn't take more than what was offered. He'd tucked her into the tent, kept his distance, was treading carefully.

Which was why she sat up and unzipped the tent.

Mase was sitting with his back propped against the log, his knees bent, and his arms folded behind his head as he stared at the sky above. The flames of the fire were lower though the clearing was pleasantly warm.

When she popped her head out of the tent, he sat upright. "You okay?" he asked.

"Yes," she said and fell silent, abruptly nervous.

She hadn't anticipated feeling awkward, but with his eyes

on her, his high cheekbones and square jaw highlighted by the fire, she found that she did.

"What is it, Sunshine?" He pushed to his feet, walked over to her, and knelt in front of the opening of the tent.

"I—" She'd made her decision, why was she so tongue-tied *now*?

"Mentally wrestling crocodiles again?"

Her throat loosened. "Something like that."

He lifted a hand and traced a finger down her cheek. "What is it?"

"I don't want you to go to sleep."

"O . . . kay." He stretched the word out, making it several syllables longer than normal. "Are you scared about being outside the shield? We can go back." He frowned. "Or I won't go to sleep?"

"No." She shook her head and flopped onto her back inside the tent, the little wink of the stars between the trees mocking her. "I'm sorry. I always do this!"

A whisper of laughter threaded its way across their mental link. "Tell men they're not allowed to sleep?"

She sat up. "Oh, shut up. I'm trying to invite you to sleep in the tent with me but as usual I've bungled the whole thing." Her eyes closed briefly in embarrassment. "I'm terrible in social situations."

A soft rustle of denim reached her ears and she peeled back her lids to find that he had crawled through the tent's opening.

"You were going to ask me to sleep with you?"

The way he said it, the soft rumble of roughened velvet coated her skin and raised the hairs on the nape of her neck.

She nodded.

A grin erupted on his face, wide and sexy as hell, and a whole lot more dangerous than the voice that made her thighs quiver. Because the feelings it invoked in her . . . wow. He was a man who could possess her heart.

Did she trust enough in the newness of their connection to hand it over?

Maybe. Maybe not.

But she did trust him enough to give herself the chance to find out.

"*Sleep,* sleep," she said, narrowing her eyes. "Don't get any ideas."

"I'm full of ideas," he teased before his face went serious. "But you do know I won't push you, right?"

"I know." She nodded, sensed his relief at the notion.

When he paused to zip up the tent, she backed up, sliding inside the sleeping bag. It was LexTal-sized, which basically meant that it dwarfed her.

With Mason sharing it, the space would be seriously reduced, but he was leaner than most of the other LexTals, so though the fit would be tight, she suspected they would manage.

Plus, it was no hardship to cuddle against him.

He closed the distance between them then waited, not moving until she lifted up the edge of the sleeping bag.

"I'm okay," she said. "Really."

After one more moment of hesitation, he slid in next to her.

They shared a few awkward minutes of trying to find a comfortable position which was only resolved when he stilled her movements and wrapped her in his arms.

She turned and buried her face into his throat, one of his biceps beneath her head, knowing she had never felt anything more wonderful than being enfolded in his warmth, covered by spicy scent.

Her heart might never be the same again.

And, shockingly, she was totally fine with that.

TWENTY

Mason

HE SWORE to himself that he wouldn't fall asleep.

But a few hours in Gabby's arms, being surrounded by her soft scent, her steady breathing, and his eyelids grew heavy. He was trained to go on very little sleep and by himself, it wouldn't have even been an issue. But the comfort, the rightness of holding her in his arms made him complacent.

He drifted off.

And . . . his memories swarmed over him, a suffocating blanket of blackness that stole every bit of joy he'd gained from being in Gabby's presence.

He was back on that rain-soaked street. The pungent smells of vomit and feces burning his nose. But he hadn't been concentrating on the scents around him. Instead, he'd been in pursuit.

Of the Dalshie.

Of one Dalshie in particular who'd enjoyed cutting and dismembering his victims. They'd eventually eliminated Jack the Ripper—as the native London dwellers had referred to him.

But the Rengalla had also suffered losses.

Mason had received a piece of intel on that rainy-London night. A note with the description of a warehouse in a seedy neighborhood. A note whose authenticity had been verified by several who lived nearby and reported suspicious activity.

He'd walked down the nearly deserted streets, ignoring the odd prostitute and shady figure that propositioned him as he moved by. He was practically in a daze, his mind so busy ferreting out a plan.

The warehouse wasn't secluded enough to completely shield their presence if a magical battle would take place, so he was trying to think through every possibility.

Mortals couldn't see their magic when the Rengalla and Dalshie used it, but they were able to see the effects of it.

And collapsing ceilings and exploding walls tended to draw attention. Not to mention the ash that coated everything and choked everyone in the vicinity when a Dalshie was killed.

Sever the head, plunge a knife into their black heart, and the Dalshie turned to dust.

There would be a lot of ash to clean up.

Of that, Mason had no doubt, but he'd still been considering strategies and wondering whether they could simply burn the evidence without risking the nearby buildings and their inhabitants when he'd arrived home. Dante and Francis would be waiting, but he had to see Victoria before he went to the warehouse. He needed to give her and Jacob a good night kiss.

It was their evening ritual, that kiss. Something he did his best to never miss, no matter how many of the enemy he was chasing.

Victoria would worry about the mission, she always did. And though Mason didn't like her to fret unnecessarily, it was nice to have someone waiting for him, caring whether he returned safely.

His love for his wife and son made him fight that much harder.

But he was so deep in thought, in planning every detail that it wasn't until he'd ascended the five steps leading up to his front door that he'd realized something was amiss.

He didn't have to turn the knob.

The door was ajar.

Utterly still silence filled the entry.

His footsteps echoed as he crossed the marble floor. The sound of his knife sliding from the scabbard in his boot startlingly loud in the quiet space.

He moved forward. Glanced into the small parlor at the front of the house.

Empty.

Then the dining room. Also empty.

The study. Victoria's private receiving rooms, the kitchen, the water closet.

Every single room was devoid of life.

But signs of his family were all around.

The fires blazing behind the grates. The half-empty cup of tea. A plate of Jacob's favorite biscuits.

Dread burned a fiery pit in Mason's stomach as he climbed the stairs to the second floor. The guest bedrooms and the nursery were as empty as the rooms on the first floor.

His and Victoria's rooms were not.

They had a small space that adjoined their separate bedrooms —though they hardly slept apart—that Victoria had lovingly decorated. In the evenings they spent many an hour playing with Jacob before he went to bed and then reading to one another once they were alone.

He hesitated with his hand on the knob, instinctively knowing he didn't want to see what was in the room and yet understanding that he must look.

The hinges creaked loudly.

Crimson soaked into the pale beige carpeting. Two pairs of blue eyes stared unseeing at the ceiling.

He woke on a gasp.

His heart pounded, sweat had soaked through his T-shirt.

Gabby stirred next to him and he knew he had to get it together or he'd risk waking her. Shifting carefully, he slid his arm from beneath her head then stroked her brow until she settled back into sleep. Once he was certain that she wouldn't wake, he crept from the tent and escaped into the clearing. Maybe two hours had passed.

The night air was heavy and damp, muffling the sounds of the nocturnal creatures, and he allowed the quiet stillness to settle his nerves. Now that the nightmare had come, it wouldn't strike again that evening.

The rest of his sleep, if he managed to grasp on to it, would be filled solely with peaceful blackness.

"Mason?"

He startled at Gabby's voice, so off his game that he hadn't even heard her or sensed she was wake.

"Go back to sleep," he whispered. "I'll be there in a second."

But the damned woman didn't oblige him.

He almost smiled, might have if he didn't have the disturbing memories circling his mind and snapping at his sanity.

"Want to talk about it?"

A laugh burst from him, all jagged glass and painful to even his own ears.

"I'll take that as a no. Here." She grabbed his hand and pulled him toward the log by the fire. "Sit," she ordered, pushing him to the ground and perching behind him on the makeshift bench. Her fingers dug into the straining muscles of his neck and shoulders, massaging deeply—and not quite comfortably.

But the hard, unrelenting motions worked.

Eventually the tightness of his muscles relaxed.

As the sting of the memories began to fade, he opened his mouth to apologize.

"Don't," she said, continuing to rub his nape.

"I—"

"*Don't*," she said again.

He nodded, didn't speak again.

And when, long minutes later, she stopped her ministrations and led him back into the tent, he followed without argument.

This time when sleep overtook him, his memories stayed locked within the deepest recesses of his mind.

"Mason?" she asked.

They were packing up their camp. Getting ready to depart for the Colony, to return to reality.

He glanced up from where he was methodically folding up the tent. "Yeah?"

"I was wondering . . ." Gabby trailed off and her cheeks went the slightest bit pink. "Daughtry told me about the waterfalls."

He felt his lips twitch at that blush. Despite everything she'd gone through, she was so damned sweet and innocent. Then he realized what she had said, and shock made him gape for a moment before he asked, "You want to go to a make out spot?"

"W-what?" Her cheeks flared fire engine bright. "I just want to see the waterfalls. Dee said they were incredible."

"I'm sure she did," he teased.

"Oh, shut up," she muttered then glanced up at him. "Is it really a make out spot?"

He waggled his brows. "What do you think?"

A sigh. "Why am I always the last one to know these things?"

The final bit of darkness from the night before faded away. He chuckled, knowing he was grinning like an idiot but unable to stop. "I'm not sure I believe that you didn't know. I think you like propositioning me. *Share my tent. Come to the waterfalls.*" He smirked. "You want me bad. *Really* bad."

Her hands plunked onto her hips. "First, you're an idiot." She huffed. "Second, yes I want you. Third, how was I supposed to know that asking to see the waterfalls was a proposition?"

He laughed, though his cock had twitched at her admission that she wanted him. Still, he was striving for light that morning, not dark, and so he continued with the teasing. "It's basically the Rengallan equivalent of 'Show me yours and I'll show you mine.'"

"What?" She cried, hands covering those pink cheeks. "Tell me you're kidding!"

"I'm kidding," he said immediately, and fought to get his smile under wraps.

"Oh. My. God." She closed her eyes. "Oh my *freaking* God. You're *not* kidding. I'm going to kill Daughtry. And Suz, for that matter."

Standing, he finished zipping the pack then slung it over his shoulder. "You're right. I'm *not* kidding, but it doesn't matter. Come on." He pulled her hands from her face and chucked her under her chin. "Let's go see those waterfalls."

TWENTY-ONE

Gabby

SHE FOLLOWED Mason down the trail, her cheeks still hot, embarrassment still coursing through her.

She considered herself a strong, independent woman, but one smile, a little good-natured teasing, and she folded like a tower of playing cards. Her spine might as well be mush. But as they made their way along the winding dirt path, crossed under low hanging branches, crunched through needles and leaves alike—well, *she* moved noisily through the forest debris, *he* was silent—her discomfort faded.

The outdoors had been her only source of pleasure from the time her father had been killed.

When her mother was distracted—with a man, with magic—Gabby would take advantage and escape into the forest surrounding their little trailer, thankful for the acres of trees between her and the next closest neighbor.

At the time, she had just been grateful for the chance to get lost, to be forgotten for a few hours to a few days.

As an adult, she was more thankful that isolation had

prevented her mother from having easy access to new victims. For whatever reason, her mother never moved them from the trailer that she'd purchased with Gabby's father.

Perhaps there *had* been an inkling of nostalgia buried deep under the black magic that coated her mother's skin.

She supposed she would never understand her mother's motivations, and she supposed . . . it didn't really matter.

"What are you thinking?" Mason murmured, pausing in his forward motion to glance back over his shoulder. "All I can sense is a thunderstorm going on in there." He leaned toward her and mock-whispered, "Please tell me that it's something involving the two of us and a sleeping bag."

She snorted. "Hush, you."

He grinned. "I'm technically the quiet triplet."

"I don't believe it," she grumbled. "You have plenty to say to me."

"That's true." He cocked his head. "But at least you're smiling now."

So she was.

"Ugh. Don't be charming," she muttered, stepping forward until she was equal with him. Her fingers found his jaw and traced across the bristly expanse, and she pressed a kiss to his cheek. "Thank you."

"Were you thinking about your mother?"

Her eyes flew up to meet his. "How?" She shook her head. She was an idiot. Their connection was stronger and— "You could hear my thoughts."

He laced his fingers with hers and pulled her forward. "Not exactly. It's more like the tenor of your thoughts change. Normally you're mind feels like sunshine"—he flashed her one of those heart-stopping grins—"all warm rays and heat. But when you think about your past . . . well, your mind gets kind of icy. Cold."

She smiled weakly. "Yikes."

"It's you," he whispered. "It's okay."

A nod and then he squeezed her fingers. They walked hand in hand for a few minutes before she said, "Your mind changes too."

"I figured," he said, nonchalant . . . or fake nonchalant, anyway.

"That's how I knew," she said. "I felt it last night. It was like our connection had been frozen in ice." Fragile, the ties between them had seemed as though they would shatter with the slightest touch.

Frustration filled him.

It was in the stiffness of his shoulders, the slight flexing of his fingers against hers, and across the link between their minds —the emotion was hot, almost scalding, and still so much better than the frigid coldness from the night before.

"I'm—"

"If you're going to apologize," she said. "Please don't. We both have things from our past that threaten to suck us under. I don't want you to feel bad just because you have a hard time forgetting those memories."

She stopped him with a tug on his hand. "If we keep moving in this direction, keep moving toward mixing our magic and invoking the bond, I don't want you to forget." Her fingers cupped his cheek. "I don't want you to forget Victoria and Jacob. They're a part of you and I'd never expect—"

"I *like* you," Mason interrupted. His voice was almost a growl, husky, and it rolled over her skin with a pleasant roughness.

He tugged her fingers off his face and pulled her close.

Irritation coursed through her.

Not because she was mad at him, but because when he held her against his chest, she couldn't reach his mouth to kiss him.

And she wanted to kiss this man, this sweet, funny man whose hazel eyes were shrouded in darkness. This man who appeared to care more about her past hurts than his own.

She wanted—

He solved the problem for her.

Reaching down, he cupped both of his hands beneath her butt and hauled her up. Her breasts pressed against his chest, and straddled his hips, felt the hard length of him between her thighs. Perfect. Fuck, that was perfect.

She threw her arms around his neck and slammed her mouth down onto his.

Heat. So much heat.

It pounded into her, little bullets of desire that penetrated the last of her fear and the tattered remains of the armor that surrounded her heart, and though she might have initiated the kiss, been the one to actually connect their mouths, but Mason was the one who jumped into the driver's seat. His tongue stroked across her lips, demanding entrance, and pushing inside to stroke against hers, nipped at her mouth, held her fiercely as he kissed and kissed and *kissed* her.

She didn't have to think, to worry she didn't know what the hell she was doing. Nothing mattered. Nothing except that it felt good to be in his arms, that she felt cherished, cared for, and so freaking turned on she wanted to—

He slowed the kiss.

Turned the deep penetrations of his tongue into smaller sips of his lips against hers, and as he pulled away from her, leaving her gasping for air, he pressed a row of kisses along her jaw and over to her ear.

"Want to see the waterfalls with me again?" he whispered.

A shocked laugh burst free, and she leaned back to see him smiling at her. His lips were slightly reddened, his breaths not completely steady either. She started to respond but he sealed his mouth to hers for a brief heat-inducing press.

"I know," he said, when he broke away and rested his forehead to hers, his spicy breath teasing her nose. "I'm a pain in the ass."

She giggled. "No pain in the ass can kiss like that."

A moment passed. She waited for Mason to release her, for them to continue walking.

He didn't.

Tilting her head back again, she glanced up into his eyes

A self-deprecating sigh escaped him. "I'm having a hard time convincing my hands to let you go."

"A *hard* time?"

They broke into peals of laughter, their breaths mingling, the happiness radiating through their mental connection buoying them both.

Eventually, he persuaded his fingers to cooperate and release her. They walked side by side down the quiet forest trail, and she couldn't help but feel hope for the first time in her life. She'd loved her father, had even loved the pieces of her mother that hadn't been tainted by the dark magic.

But she'd never expected to love a man. Wasn't sure that she would ever be able to expose herself so readily.

The vulnerability, the risk—

No.

She hadn't ever thought she would able to do that.

Mason made her think she could.

"What does a LexTal do anyway?" she asked a little while later. She could hear the waterfalls ahead, the slapping sound of water against rocks, the faint roar of the downward rushing liquid.

He turned to face her. "You already know what we do."

She huffed out a sigh. "No, what I know is that Morgan"—his brother—"says your job is to stop people from being stupid." Mason snorted and she continued, "I know you *fight* for us. But what does that mean on a day to day basis?"

He grabbed her hand and tugged her forward. It was a few minutes before he replied but she didn't push, since she could actually feel his mind considering her question and formulating the answer.

Perhaps bonding had been biology's way of teaching women patience.

Her lips twitched and Mason chuckled.

"Probably not," he said, shrugging when she glanced at him in surprise. "Got that thought loud and clear."

She was starting to understand what Dee had meant about the bond having its own set of drawbacks—the potential for embarrassing or uncomfortable things to be overheard was a big one. This time it wasn't bad. But what about those inner, unkind thoughts people had about one another? The mean little quips that most would never, *ever* say aloud?

If they did this bonding thing, she would need to talk to Daughtry about finding a way to ensure some privacy for both her and Mason.

"Not touching *that* comment on woman," he said, lightly. "The LexTals help with patrols and go on missions to find, well . . . you know what John does."

She nodded. John was really good at finding those who'd slipped through the cracks. Like her.

"The rest of us train the lower ranks of soldiers, teach classes for the civilians—Suz has convinced Monroe to start giving a self-defense class for the females of the Colony."

Her lips twitched at the thought of Mason's stoic brother teaching a class full of women. "And what do you do?"

"Mostly monitoring," he answered. "I run all of the surveillance and security. I schedule shifts for patrols, make sure all the defenses are functioning." He shrugged. "It's mostly computer work."

"Sounds important."

He pushed a branch out of the way, and she ducked underneath it. After he'd come through, he crouched slightly and met her eyes. "Everyone's job at the Colony is."

Her heart squeezed hard.

She wouldn't say it out loud—and would attempt to keep the thought in her own mind—but the man was beyond sweet.

As they walked on, the sound of the waterfalls increased, and she had to raise her voice to be heard. "You spend a lot of time on the computer?"

He nodded. "Lots of cameras to monitor."

Mischievousness chased the warm bubbly feeling within her. "That must be why you're so out of shape."

That dumbfounded him. She could feel it, witnessed it in the slackening of his jaw and the furrowing of his brow. He glanced down at the six feet plus of hardened muscles, of narrow hips and flat abs, then looked back up at her.

"Out of shape?" he asked.

She giggled, couldn't stop it.

An almost predatory look came into his eyes at the sound. It raised goosebumps on her nape, her arms.

Affecting a sad, false pout, she walked toward him. "Poor man, doesn't get out much. Doesn't get to exercise his LexTal skills." She wasn't entirely sure what had made her feel so playful. Maybe it was the earlier hope. Or perhaps, it was just being with him, having him tease her. Either way, she didn't care.

For the first time in ages, she felt right. Like she was a

twenty-something woman who could play and have fun, not an ancient old crone who couldn't risk opening her heart even one millimeter.

"*My* LexTal skills?" he asked, his tone taking on a warning edge that made her grin.

"Yup. They're sorely lacking. In fact, I bet I can beat you to the waterfalls." She plunked her hands on her hips. "Unless you're too scared?"

He raised a brow. "Did you just give me the equivalent of a schoolyard challenge?"

She didn't let the fact that she'd never set foot on a schoolyard dampen her spirits. "I believe I did."

Amusement crept into hazel eyes. "All right then. I see I have something to prove. What are your terms, Sunshine?"

She considered that for a moment, not having thought that far ahead in her silliness. "I win and you have to bring me coffee first thing in the morning every day for a week."

The predatory gleam was back. "Is that supposed to be a punishment? Having to see you every day?" His teeth flashed when she sputtered. "And what do I get when I beat you?"

"Don't you mean *if?*" she retorted.

"No." He stepped very close, not quite touching, but near enough that she could feel the heat of him even through their layers of clothes. "I mean *when.*"

She didn't stop to wonder why that sexy rasp and towering stance was sexy on Mason when it had been disturbing on her mother's men. All she knew was that he didn't make her feel threatened. That if she asked him to back off, to give her space, he would do it without a moment's hesitation or a single protest.

"Well, I guess *if* you win," she murmured. "Then I'll show you *my* waterfalls."

"What exactly"—his gaze flicked down and back up—"are your waterfalls?"

She froze, wondering at that too. Then lifted her chin and smiled at him. "I'll just call it . . . dealer's choice."

Molten heat darkened the brown threads in his hazel eyes, making them almost black with desire. "Then I guess I'd better win."

Her body agreed wholeheartedly with that statement.

"Okay," she said, sucking in a breath, readying herself. Trying damned hard to focus on the challenge. It had been her idea, but now she wasn't sure she wanted to leave Mason at all. In fact, she was positive that she wanted to stay here and—

The swat on her but made her squawk.

"Go on then," he said. "I'll give you a five-minute head start." His eyes smoldered down at her. "After which you can show me those waterfalls."

She swallowed against a suddenly dry throat, against the intense need to claim this funny, sweet, teasing man. That urge to bond, to forget the challenge, to just get naked and launch herself at him was nearly overwhelming.

But she'd found her spine, and she was keeping it.

"You can't use your sneaky bond skills. Or teleport to the falls."

"I won't cheat," he murmured. "Eyes and ears and nose only. No magic."

A brusque nod. "Good."

"Good." He smiled and it held a wicked gleam. "Go on then. Oh, Sunshine?" He called just as she'd stepped through the tree line, his voice serious rather than laughing. "Make sure you take the right fork at the path just ahead. That's the one that leads to the falls."

She nodded her assurance then continued forward, and the moment she was around the corner, she started sprinting.

Her heart pounded and her palms were sweaty. But not in fear.

In excitement. In anticipation.

When she reached the fork, she took the right path as Mason had instructed.

The trees swallowed her whole and the sound of the falls pounding against the rocks below made her ears ring.

TWENTY-TWO

Mason

PRECISELY FIVE MINUTES LATER, he headed down the trail. Gabby's path was ridiculously easy to track, everything from her obvious footprints in the moist dirt, to the disturbed leaves and bushes, the broken branches.

She may as well have been a herd of elephants, her route was so clear.

At the fork, he breathed out a small sigh of relief in seeing that she had taken the correct turn off. Then he closed his mind and opened his eyes and ears and nose to the space around him.

If he concentrated, he could still smell her in the air—the slight tang of citrus, the soft floral note of lavender.

The waterfall was loud, a roaring, crashing noise that dampened his well-trained hearing, forced him to rely on his eyes.

She had slowed midway along the trail. As he followed, closing the distance between them easily, he decided that he needed to ask her if she'd slowed because she'd gotten tired or if she'd just wanted him to catch her.

If she'd been anxious to show him *her* waterfall.

Grinning and picking up his pace, he flowed through the woods, not even realizing that he'd activated his magic until a glimmer of sunlight reflected off the threads of power surrounding him and blinded him.

Taking a breath, he cut off the flow, tucked his magic back into the space in his mind. Since his specialty was teleportation, he possessed the ability to bend air to his will. He could use that to move across distances faster than the eye could see. In fact, he had the feeling that if they were fully bonded, and he called upon his capacity to teleport, he could be in front of her in the space of a few moments.

But he'd promised not to cheat, so he held back the urge and tracked her the old-fashioned way.

Which was probably the only reason he spotted the anomaly in the first place.

It began as only a peculiar sense in the back of his mind. Then continued as he saw a few broken branches that weren't consistent with her path. Never one to ignore his instincts, her picked up the pace.

The next thing he noticed was the shortening of the distance between Gabby's footprints—an indication she'd begun moving faster.

Breaking his promise to her was easy at that point, because if she'd suddenly walked quicker, if she'd *run* from something that wasn't him . . . his promise meant nothing when compared to her safety.

Adrenaline pumped through his body.

It fueled his magic, helped him go faster, to process the sensory input more quickly. The threads of power wrapping around him were crisp and competent as they lifted him slightly —thus reducing his friction, allowing him to run faster—and propelled him through the forest.

She was close, he could feel her presence growing larger in

his consciousness, but she wasn't close enough to discern her exact location. Not without them being bonded.

In fact, he was concentrating so hard on the feel of her, on the feel of her *fear* in his mind, that he almost missed it.

Wrenching off his magic, he skidded to a stop.

There were drag marks that led to the right, into the thick vegetation just off the trail. Someone had attempted to cover them hastily with a pile of sticks and leaves.

He bent, saw that the forced path continued into the underbrush.

Ahead a single pair of footprints continued on—wider, longer than those that had belonged to Gabby.

A pathetic effort at disguise. A method that surely anyone would see through.

But what did it *mean*?

She wouldn't have gone to these lengths to win. For one, she didn't have the skill. For another, she wouldn't have made him think that she was in danger.

That was when he heard it.

The scuff of a sneaker against stone. The softest whimper, muffled, barely audible. Without thinking, he shot down the path, faster than most people's eyes would have been able to process.

He reached the falls seconds later.

And was utterly horrified at the sight in front of him.

Four Dalshie were gathered around Gabby, who was on her side, her knees curled to her chest, her arms covering her head. They stood on the narrow outcropping, a flat expanse of granite where lovebirds usually brought their blankets and picnicked before the falls. The Dalshie crowded close, an occasional black strand of magic snapping from their palms and flicking in her direction. He could hear their laughter when she screamed and squirmed away from the cutting, dark power.

He didn't think.

Just moved—crouching to yank his knife from the holster on his ankle and dropping the pack from his back in one smooth movement.

It hit the ground with a soft *thunk*.

One of the Dalshie drew back and kicked Gabby hard.

She cried out—a jarring, brutal sound that at once eviscerated him and filled him with such rage that he had closed the distance between himself and the group before his next heartbeat. His knife's blade met the flesh of the nearest Dalshie, penetrated its heart with a long, sure stroke.

Ash filled the air.

He ignored the distraction and turned to face the remaining Dalshie.

They attacked him at once. He managed to block one, to wound another, but the strike from behind took him by surprise —a strand of black magic wrapped around one thigh, knocking him to his knees, cutting through his jeans and sending warm blood freely flowing down his leg.

Gabby screamed, but aside from one quick glance that assured him she was okay, he couldn't focus on her.

Not if he wanted to survive. Not if he wanted to ensure she lived.

He shot his own magic behind him, a hardened bolt of fire. It wouldn't kill the Dalshie, but it would wound and force his attacker to take a moment to heal.

That distraction was what Mason was after.

It worked. A curse blistered through the air and the black magic that had wrapped around his thigh disappeared. A second later, he was back on his feet and charging at the nearest Dalshie.

This time he managed to deal the killing blow—a slice across the throat, severing his enemy's head from his shoulders.

More ash coated the air, made the stones at his feet slippery.

When the black magic came again, this time Mason was ready, already turning, already facing the two enemies at his back. He dodged, using his ability to teleport, and flew forward to thrust his knife directly between the closer Dalshie's ribs.

One to go.

Spitting out the sickening remains that clogged his nose, coated his mouth and tongue, he risked a glance at Gabby.

Only to find that she wasn't there.

"Mason!" The fear in her voice, slamming across their connection focused his mind like a laser.

His magic surged, readying to teleport toward her when the masculine voice rang out.

"Stop, or I'll kill her."

They would kill her anyway. They always did. But even as his adrenaline was surging, memories and the present in his brain, Mason's eyes finally caught up with his mind. The final Dalshie stood at the cliff's edge, his arm around Gabby's throat, a narrow slice of his chest unprotected and vulnerable to a killing blow.

Mason didn't stop to think.

In one swift movement, the blade flew from his hand and he teleported himself forward.

It was too late.

The Dalshie pushed Gabby hard. She slipped on the wet surface, scrambled to stay on her feet, and . . . with a shriek of terror, she went over the edge.

Was lost beneath the millions of gallons of pounding water.

The Dalshie rotated back to Mason, his shit-eating grin spreading his fetid lips wide.

Not for long.

The knife sunk into the Dalshie's chest. Ash exploded.

Mason didn't care about any of that.
He threw himself over the cliff.

TWENTY-THREE

Gabby

HER SCREAM CUT OFF ABRUPTLY.

One second she was plummeting through the air, her eyes shut, water pounding into her hard enough to bruise. The next she was wrapped in a pair of strong arms and floating in space.

She didn't need to smell the spicy scent of sandalwood or to see the firm jaw and hazel eyes to know it was Mason.

No, she'd already known that he would save her. Known it with bone-deep certainty.

Slowly, they began to rise.

She wrapped her arms and legs around him, holding tight as they climbed the distance she'd fallen.

It was a long way.

"I've got you." His voice was soft, comforting, but his mind was a mess—a tangled web of anger, fear, rage, and the frozen quality that it took on whenever his memories got particularly bad. Opening her eyes, she stared into his, willing him to feel that she was okay, that she was so thankful he'd saved her, to not blame himself.

It was too late.

He wasn't shut off from her. Not exactly. But he sure as hell wasn't receptive to her gratitude.

Glancing away, her jaw dropped open at the utter beauty of his magic. It surrounded them in a web of green and gold and brown, an exact match to the ever-changing mix of colors that were his irises.

A moment later, they were at the top of the falls, and back on the flat granite surface.

He unwove his magic enough to slip one arm through—snatched up the backpack—then closed the hole and propelled them forward. They rose above the trees and flew in the direction of the Colony, toward the pearlescent shield of intertwined emerald and violet fibers. It was bright despite the several-mile distance.

And . . . it took *maybe* ten seconds to get there.

Maybe.

If she were rounding up.

Because even as she processed the sheer speed at which they were traveling, in the next heartbeat, she found herself on her feet, planted on the grass outside the shield, Mason steadying her as he unzipped the pack and pulling out her phone.

He punched a series of numbers into it and began barking orders.

A minute later, the shield peeled back enough that they were able to enter. The door-sized opening began to close even before they were fully through. Dante, Cody, John, and Daughtry poured out of the front of the Colony, followed by Suz and a few of the other nurses, and Gabby knew her internal limit was surpassed.

She knew *all* about adrenaline, knew the aftereffects were leaving her shaky and light-headed. She needed . . .

"*Mason.*"

It wasn't until he turned surprised hazel eyes on her that she realized he'd heard her mental plea clearly, hadn't just sensed her emotions and faced her.

No, he'd actually *heard* her. From her mind to his. Happiness and fear chased through her, followed by a hundred other emotions, but by then it was too late to process them.

Black spots marred her vision and unconsciousness took her under.

WHEN SHE WOKE UP, her head was pounding, her eyes crusted shut. She was in bed, a thin blanket pulled up to her neck.

The room was dark, seeming as though it were filled solely with shadows.

Then one of the shadows moved.

Her gasp halted mid-release. Because she knew that mind, had sensed the warmth, the rightness of being near the man in the room.

"Are you okay?" she asked, her throat dry, her voice rasping.

A lamp flicked on, and she blinked, realizing for the first time that she wasn't in the infirmary as she'd expected but in someone's quarters.

Someone's because this sure as hell wasn't *her* room.

She watched as Mason turned and opened a door. The sound of running water filled the space, evoking all sorts of memories that she didn't want to remember.

Roaring falls. Her stomach feeling as though it would fly up and out her throat.

But underneath that had been conviction.

Not that she was going to die.

No, she'd *known* that Mason would save her. Now she just had to convince him to not blame himself—

A cool glass was pressed into her hand. "Drink."

Her fingers closed reflexively around it then lifted it to her mouth and she guzzled hurriedly. After the cup was drained and her throat no longer burned, she turned to Mason.

"Come here," she murmured, holding out her arms.

The demons were back, had ensnared his mind in frost. As much as it pained her to let him stew, she knew that right now wasn't the time for assurances or to try to ferret out every single facet of his emotions.

Nope. This was the time to let him hold her, to let him *feel* she was whole and safe and uninjured.

When he hesitated, she pulled out the big guns.

"I need you."

He closed the distance between them, pausing for a moment near the side of the bed to remove his boots. The mattress dipped under his weight and sandalwood coated her nostrils as he lay down and tugged her into his arms.

She wasn't tired. Couldn't possibly sleep more than she already had.

But a few minutes in Mason's arms, his warmth soaking into her, the steady beat of his heart beneath her ear, and her eyes were drifting closed.

"Rest now," he murmured.

"Not tired—" The protest was punctuated by a wide yawn and she felt the first tendrils of amusement crack through the ice that encased Mason's mind.

The glimpse of emotions she was able to sense below that ice scared her.

A whirling, tangled mass of thoughts, of guilt and anger, of *fear* assaulted her for one long second before he was able to lock everything away.

"You shouldn't feel—"

"Hush," he whispered. "It'll be better in the morning."

She wanted to protest, but he was stroking a hand through her hair and down her back, murmuring soft comforts in her ear and sleep snagged its talons into her.

When she next awoke, Mason was gone.

"Hey!"

Turning, she spotted Daughtry running towards her.

Before she had the chance to do more than smile, she was wrapped tight into her friend's arms.

"I'm so glad you're okay," Dee murmured, giving Gabby one last squeeze before letting go. Her friend's cheeks were a little pink and she shrugged awkwardly. "Sorry about the hug." She grimaced. "You had me worried."

"Because I fell off a waterfall, or because I ran away like a little kid?"

"Either." Dee grinned. "Okay, both."

Gabby felt amusement course through her for the first time that day, for the first time since she'd woken in Mason's quarters and had found him gone. The mattress cold, his scent already dissipating.

"Oh, shut up," she said. "And come here." Reaching forward, she snagged her friend in another hug, longer and less awkward the second go around. Neither of them were big touchers, but damned if this situation didn't call for a little more hugging.

A wolf-whistle broke them apart.

"Don't move!" the masculine voice called. "I left my phone in my quarters—"

"Shut up, Tyler!" they said in unison.

"I'm wounded," he said, moving down the hall and around the corner. A heartbeat later, he peeked back around the corner and called, "Seriously, though. Suz was looking for you, Gabby baby. She's in the infirmary."

Gabby baby?

She shook herself, ignoring the nickname and focused on the more important piece of that statement. "Is everything okay?"

Tyler nodded, turning his smile on her, the light from the crystal chandeliers glinting against his skin. "Apparently you have some computer work to catch up on."

Gabby laughed to herself, that reminding her of the joking conversation she'd had the previous day with Mason about his job.

Computer work.

Apparently both of them were at risk of getting out of shape.

When Tyler looked at her knowingly, she bit her lip to stifle her amusement and quickly waved goodbye. Turning back to Daughtry—who was staring at her with a mix of concern and cat-ate-the-canary on her face—Gabby scrambled for an excuse to get away.

It wasn't that she didn't want to confide in her friend.

It was that she didn't know what was going on.

Mason was there. He was gone.

Aside from checking in with Suz and her *computer work,* Gabby knew she needed to track down Mason. His mind was a faint presence in the back of hers, a light buzz that told her he was alive, uninjured, but it didn't tell her anything about how he was feeling. It didn't let her know if he was still wracked with guilt, still trapped beneath the frigidness of the past.

So yes, he was right up there at the top of her list of priorities.

An excuse readied on the tip of her tongue, Gabby started to speak, "I—"

"Before you put your running skills to use and scoot out of here," Dee said, grabbing her arm and turning them both in the direction of the infirmary. Her voice lowered. "Is it true? Did you . . . bond?"

"I—" Gabby scrambled. "Why would you—?"

"Mason went on a rampage last night, demanded that you be taken to his quarters, that he look after you." Dee shrugged. "Cody said Mason looked how he felt when all of the bonding stuff was going on with us."

Gabby's feet froze for a half a second before she was able to get them moving again. "I—uh—we're not bonded."

A look of such disappointment passed across Dee's face that Gabby instantly felt guilty enough to spill the truth. Despite the urge to hold the truth close to her chest, to not let anyone know in case things didn't work out, she couldn't lie to her friend.

"Dee?"

Daughtry glanced over.

"We're not bonded." She sucked in a breath and blurted, "Yet."

"What?" Daughtry screeched then winced and lowered her voice. "Yet? *Yet?* Tell me!" she demanded. "Tell me everything!"

"I—"

"No, wait." Daughtry put her hand up, bringing that side of the conversation to a dizzying halt. "I'm being nosy. Don't feel like you have to say anything. I know it's unexpected and you're probably feeling rubbed raw on the inside."

She studied her friend's face, soaked up the words that perfectly described the way she was feeling. Then noted the puppy dog *please tell me every single detail* expression in Dee's startlingly violet eyes.

"Good grief," Gabby muttered. "You're just as bad as the rest of them."

Daughtry had the good sense to look abashed. "I'm sorry." She winced. "Okay, I'm really not. Apparently, my inner busy-body has come out to roost. I *want* to know," she said. "The difference is that I don't *expect* you to tell me." Her cheeks went a little pink. "Okay, maybe I do."

There was a moment of silence before they both burst into laughter.

Gabby shook her head. "What am I going to do with you, huh?"

"No clue," Daughtry joked but then her expression sobered. "Baring your soul or not, are you really doing okay?"

She shrugged and they turned another corner, this one leading into the hall by the infirmary. "I'm okay," she said. "I'm shocked, of course. It's not like I could have ever expected this."

"Can I just say that it'll be nice to not be the only bonded couple?"

A smile curled Gabby's lips. "Yes, you can. But I'm not sure when we'll bond." *Or if,* she thought, sobering, considering the way his mind currently felt where it brushed against hers. Cold. Distant. And beneath that, guilt and pain. "We're taking it slow, getting to know each other before we commit to the whole life-altering, magical connection thing." Her tone was deliberately light.

Daughtry smiled, though it was tinged with concern. "That's smart, though," she said. "I know it would have been nice to have that option, to have not mixed our magic until we'd understood the consequences. Not that I regret any of my time with Cody," she added hurriedly. "It was just a big adjustment all at once."

Considering that Dee hadn't grown up in the Colony, hadn't known about her magic at until just before she'd fled the

Dalshie invading her home and met up with Cody and John, Gabby could well understand her friend's reasoning.

She shrugged. "It's all worked out now." A peaceful, glazed-over expression came over her friend's face—*Cody drunk* again—and Gabby's heart did a little flip. She might have that with Mason, that connection, the lacing together of each other's souls, the love and devotion.

Dee blinked and a wry smile came over her face. "Sorry," she said. "I need to go."

"Cody back from patrol?"

Daughtry's cheeks heated. "Maybe."

Gabby laughed and gave her friend a little shove. "Go on then."

Dee nodded but hesitated before she would have turned away. "Hey, Gabby? I think you're smart to take things slow, to learn each other before becoming bound as tight as two souls can be." She paused, as if trying to find the correct words. "But don't be afraid to jump. Because eventually one of you will have to."

TWENTY-FOUR

Mason

HE WAS IN HELL.

The past tangled with the present, images of Victoria and Jacob intertwined with the vision of Gabby being pushed from the cliff. When he'd propelled himself from the side he hadn't been thinking, had only been able to see the fear in her face, hear her scream of terror.

It had been everything that he'd pictured Victoria and Jacob experiencing—the visual representation of his deepest, darkest fears.

But much worse. It had been so much worse than he'd imagined.

So he did what he always did.

Went and shot shit.

The familiar weight of the gun in his hand was soothing; the rapid *pop-pop* sound of the shots—muted through his headphones—matched his elevated pulse.

His skin was too tight for his body, the memories threatened to consume him.

"Fuck!"

He dropped the spent gun to the counter. It hit with a *smack* that echoed the sound of his fist crunching against the concrete wall on his left side. Blood dripped from his split knuckles, and he knew that later it would hurt like hell.

But right at that moment, it was the demons inside of him that were threatening to consume him whole and not the pain in his hand.

Rage and fear burned hot within him.

Why, when he'd finally accepted that he might be able to move forward, to risk his heart enough to build something with Gabby, had the Dalshie come in and screwed everything up again?

He wanted to go out and kill each and every one of them. He wanted to bathe in their ashes, to have the substance coat his skin like it was some sort of sick battle trophy. He—

"That good, huh, bro?"

Mason's eyes slid closed at his brother's voice. "What do you want?"

Morgan—the youngest of the three of them by about ten minutes—leaned around Mason, and though he smiled, his eyes were serious as they took in all the details. Spent casings, discarded magazines, the gun placed haphazardly on the counter. "You're scaring the new recruits."

Mason rolled his eyes but flashed his gaze to the space over Morgan's shoulder. A group of four or five Rengallan warriors were standing there, and they looked—a curse hissed out from between his clenched teeth—terrified, all huddled together in the corner.

"Dante has his work cut out with those ones," he muttered, throwing the bait out there in a lame attempt to get Morgan to change the subject.

It didn't work.

"We were no different at their age. Look at them. They can't be more than twenty." Morgan ran a hand through his hair then focused fully on Mason. "Want to tell me why you insist on self-medicating with bullets instead of alcohol like a normal person?"

"I'm not self-medicating anything." As denials went, it was pretty pathetic, but Mason went with it anyway. Turning back to the counter, he began gathering the empty magazines and picked up the gun. The he walked to the wide bank of shelving at the back of the armory and pulled out the necessary supplies to clean and reload the everything.

LexTals cleaned up after themselves.

It was one of the first thing they'd been taught. Replace what was used, leave everything ready in case of an attack.

Morgan—the persistent bastard—followed him, snatching up the box of bullets and grabbing the magazines to reload before Mason could protest. Side by side, they worked in silence, Morgan seemingly relaxed and Mason's spine winding tighter with each passing moment. He kept glancing up, expecting his brother to take advantage and start questioning.

Morgan didn't.

Eventually, Mason was able to concentrate fully on the task in front of him. Clearing out the gunpowder, oiling all the respective parts. He controlled the things he could, ensured that everything would function properly. It all worked better if he—

"Does the self-medicating have anything to do with a certain curvy-as-hell, delicious receptionist you ran off with?" Morgan asked, continuing their earlier conversation as if they hadn't been silent for the last fifteen minutes. The tone was mild, his eyes too wide to be anything but false innocence.

Mason swallowed back a growl, wanting to tear into his

brother for daring to look at Gabby, for talking about her gorgeous body. "I didn't run off with anyone."

"How about spent the night with?" Morgan pressed.

Clenching his jaw, Mason didn't answer, just forced himself to concentrate on the task at hand. When he'd finished with the gun, he hung it back on the rack with the others. Morgan, proving that he was somehow smarter than common society might expect, fell silent, and wordlessly returned the filled magazines to their proper container.

Or maybe not.

Because as they walked side by side out of the armory, Morgan bumped his shoulder and said, "That Gabby has the sweetest ass I've ever seen. I'd like to—"

Mason reacted before his brain had fully processed it was crap that Morgan was spouting. In one smooth movement, he had his brother pinned against the wall, his forearm digging roughly into the soft flesh of Morgan's neck.

And his moronic brother was grinning like a fool.

"You're so screwed," Morgan rasped out. "You haven't tried to punch me since . . ." The smile flattened out, the unspoken reference to Victoria sobering his brother's amusement.

Mason let him go with a curse. Then turned and walked in the direction of his quarters. He needed a shower and—dammit —he needed to find Gabby, to see her. The feelings threatened to surge again. His fear that he wouldn't be able to keep her safe, that he should give up now before he risked her safety.

Before he was shattered into pieces that couldn't be glued back together.

He forced the emotions back. Their connection was still strengthening, their shared time making it almost impossible to turn away from the link tying them together.

And deep down, he didn't want to turn away.

He didn't trust anyone else to keep her safe.

Yes.

But also, it wasn't just that he wanted to protect her. He liked Gabby. He enjoyed spending time with her, thought she was gorgeous and cute and sexy and incredibly strong. It was just that—

"She's not Victoria," Morgan said, interrupting Mason's thoughts.

Turning to his brother, surprise coursing through him at the nearly telepathic insight. Quickly, he shoved it away. Morgan had always been able to see through him, more so than any other person.

It shouldn't surprise him that his own brother understood him so well.

"I *know* that she's not Victoria," he said and sighed. "It should bother me more than it does, I think. But it doesn't matter to me that Gabby is different."

She was strong in ways Victoria had never been. She challenged him, pushed back. She was unique . . . which meant she could possess a completely different portion of his heart.

Wonderful. Terrifying.

"She's great," Mason said when Morgan didn't speak. "I like her a lot." He paused and cursed under her breath. "Maybe too much," he added softly. Frustration fueled his steps as he began walking again. Everything in his mind was snarled, but he was too old to let fears rule him.

And he was too damned old to be hurt again. To be shattered into a million pieces.

"What the hell does that mean?" Morgan asked, easily keeping pace.

"I don't know."

"You *don't* know?" Morgan grabbed his arm and wrenched

him to a halt. "You say you like this woman. For the first time in almost *two centuries* you feel something for a woman and you're wavering." He shoved Mason. Hard. "Go *after* her, bro. Don't just stand there too scared to jump in from the sidelines."

"We're bonded."

Morgan's arm dropped. "What?"

"Gabby and I are bonded." Mason paused, starting forward again as the words flowed out. "Or almost bonded. We haven't mixed our magic but everything else is there. The mental link, the possessiveness. I've even heard her." He tapped his temple. "I heard her mind in my own. And fuck, Morgan, I could tell you exactly where she is right now."

"I—holy shit." His brother fumbled for a few seconds then shook his head, as though clearing it. "But that's good news, right? A bond is a *good* thing."

Was it?

Mason supposed on the surface it was. But all of the bullshit tearing through his mind gave him pause.

"I'm not sure."

"Daughtry and Cody are sickeningly happy."

"Yeah." He released a long, slow breath. "But I'm not Cody."

"And Daughtry's not Gabby," Morgan said. "That's the point. A bond isn't just about creating little magical geniuses, like Daughtry says. It's about bringing out the best in one another."

He shook his head. "I don't know about that. Everything I've ever read says a bond is biology and nothing more."

Morgan sighed. "Maybe I'm as much of a sap as Cody, but I can't believe that."

"Why not?"

"Why not believe it's only biology?" his brother asked. "Because if our existence is solely reduced to making babies to populate the earth in the future, then I'm opting out." Morgan poked him in the chest. "I want to *live*, bro. I want to have a woman I can laugh with and love and be pissed at then make up. And then I want to do the whole damned thing again."

"Sounds exhausting," Mason quipped. Though he would never admit it—even under pain of death—the picture his brother painted was appealing. So damned appealing he could almost imagine the entire scenario with Gabby.

Her cheeks would be glazed with pink in frustration, her brown eyes filled with sparks. She'd be beautiful and sexy and—

Damn.

Forget the fact that his brother may be way more insightful than he'd ever given him credit for, Mason wanted *that*.

He wanted a chance at a future with Gabby more than he wanted his next breath.

"Whatever you say, bro." Morgan tilted his head to the opposite hall. "I'm going to crash now."

Mason frowned. "Did you cover John's patrol last night?"

Morgan nodded. "John got a tip he wanted to check out. Monroe teleported him there and back." He shrugged. "Turned out it was nothing."

"Don't forget to eat."

Morgan grinned, a quick flash of white teeth. "Mom already dropped off a plate for me." He narrowed his eyes and affected a terrible version of their mother's voice. "She expects to see you for dinner."

Mason groaned as he turned toward his own quarters, Morgan's laughter chasing him all the way down the hall.

Their mother was great. But being called to dinner meant one of two things. She needed a favor—usually involving painting the walls or rearranging every single bit of furniture in her rooms—or they were being called in to be interrogated.

And even the most experienced FBI investigator had nothing on their mother.

As Mason stripped off his clothes and stepped into the shower to wash the smell of sweat and gunpowder down the drain, he knew his mother wasn't readying to redesign her quarters again.

Nope. This was about Gabby.

TWENTY-FIVE

Gabby

SHE STARED out the open door of her quarters with surprise. Mason's hair was damp from the shower and he wore a button-down and slacks.

She'd never seen him in anything aside from a T-shirt and jeans.

The look was a good one.

"So will you come?" he asked into the silence. His request, blurted the moment she'd opened the door, had surprised her and then she'd gotten distracted by his shoulders, his chest—

"You want me to meet your mother?" It was a squeak, rather than a normal reply. "Now?"

His eyes danced with amusement. "Yes."

Her heart pounded and her words were as hurried as the thoughts racing across her mind. "But what should I wear? I need time to shower and do my hair and—"

His fingers grazed her cheek. "I was married, Sunshine. I know you need some time. It's not for an hour." He stepped into her space, forcing her to either retreat or have him press against her.

As much as the idea of having all of his hard muscles flush against her body appealed to her, they didn't have time for that. Not if she was going to make a good impression on his mother.

Oh God, was she actually going to do this? Meet. His. *Mother?*

No.

"I—" She began then shook her head. "I—uh . . ."

"Just say yes," he murmured. "If you don't, I'll spend the whole time fielding questions about you. She might as well have the answers from the source, don't you think?"

"Why would she—?" She broke off. "She knows. *Already?* But how?"

His lips twitched. "Have you forgotten where you live?"

She shook her head. "No." She really shouldn't be surprised that his mother had heard. The Rengalla exchanged gossip like it was an actual currency. Not that they were mean. Their involvement came from the fact that they were all nosy busybodies. "You all need to get better things to do," she muttered.

He smiled fully then. "Tell me about it." He bent and pressed one long kiss to her mouth—lips closed, to her disappointment. "So you'll come?"

She sighed. "I'll come." But as she turned away, a whiff of frost crossed her mind. "Are you okay?"

Outwardly, he seemed normal. But his mind held the slightest trace of cold—a thin vein of ice that made her leery. As though his entire persona were only an act. As though he was simply going through the motions.

She didn't like *that* at all.

"I'm fine." There was an edge to those words that made her pause, that brought every bit of caution she'd fostered in the relationship with her mother to the surface.

The instinct to avoid the conflict was great.

Her feelings for Mason were stronger.

And the man in front of her *was* Mason, not a cold-eyed, grabby-handed bastard who wanted something from her she wasn't willing to give.

He'd saved her life. Promised to go slow despite the fact that his urge to bond with her was intense. He was the man who'd listened to her deepest, darkest secrets and hadn't batted an eye.

The man who had accepted her—oozing wounds of the past and all.

"You're not fine." Her voice was strong, she thought, not revealing the warnings interspersed in her mind.

She wished she could say she was absolutely certain that he wouldn't turn away from her, wouldn't hurt her, but that wasn't entirely true. She trusted him, had faith in him, but those feelings were newly grown. One didn't just shed off the hurts of the past in an instant. It was a slow metamorphosis—a caterpillar transforming into a butterfly. So, although she hoped she was right, that hope was a fragile thing. A sharp word from Mason and she would crumble—

No. Fuck that. She wouldn't crumble.

She was smarter, *tougher* than that little girl of her past— and that little girl had been damned strong. To survive what she had, to come through the darkness relatively unscathed, she'd had to be.

Strength wasn't the issue.

Instead, it was whether or not she would ever be able to open up enough to put her heart into someone else's hands.

"Gabby."

Her name was a soft whisper of sound in the space between them. Mason speaking didn't surprise her. Rather, it was the wealth of feeling in the five letters of her name.

Affection. Anger. Pride. Concern. Sadness.

Those emotions spread across the link of their minds—a woven tapestry of twisted thoughts and untried fondness.

"I'm fine," he repeated.

"No," she said, stepping right up to him, crowding him in the narrow entryway of her quarters. They'd moved all but five feet from the door, but she vowed right then that she wouldn't take another freaking step until he told her what was the matter. "You're not okay."

Her chin lifted, her feet spread as she barred the exit. If he wanted to avoid the issue, he'd have to go through her.

But he wouldn't do that.

Because he wouldn't hurt her.

She straightened her shoulders. "You're not fine or all right or *okay*. No," she said, when she felt the protest well up. "There's something eating at you, something big, something destructive, and I don't like it. So either own up and tell me what it is or stop letting it destroy you."

Silence, heavy, *heavy* silence stretched between them for a long, uneasy moment.

He stared at her, his hazel eyes unfathomable as his mind became so tangled and snarled that she couldn't discern a single feeling.

Then the corner of his mouth popped up.

His mind cleared.

And the frost, the icicles that had been threatening to dislodge and impale them both, disappeared, laughter taking their place. It tinkled across their connection, lightened his eyes.

He reached across the few inches of space between them and tenderly cupped her cheek. "Oh, Sunshine," he murmured.

His forehead rested on hers, his free hand came up to the other side of her face, and they stayed like that for a long time, the moment stretching until the closeness of the contact, of their bodies and minds made her eyes sting.

Blinking against the sudden intimacy but relieved that Mason's mind was no longer clogged with ice, she stepped back. "I'll go get changed."

He leaned in, ran his thumb across the skin beneath her lashes, and wiped away moisture she hadn't realized was there.

She watched, mesmerized, as he lifted his thumb to his mouth. "You taste like you smell—floral and tart," he said, his voice rough. "It's sexy as hell. And too damned distracting."

"That's a bad thing?" she asked, the question wobbling the slightest bit as desire flooded through her. It made her thighs clench, her lips tingle in anticipation.

For good reason, it seemed. Because barely had the words left her mouth and he was bending and slanting his mouth across hers.

Heat.

So much heat with such little contact.

Mason's hands weren't even *on* her, his body held away from hers. The scorching hotness came only from his mouth.

It was spectacular.

She found herself leaning closer, eliminating the distance between them, wanting the contact of his hard chest against hers. She needed to feel the physical proof of his arousal, to press every inch of her body to his. But the moment her breasts brushed against his front, he groaned and pulled back.

"Gabby," he warned and tried to back away.

She ignored that, lacing her hands around his neck, attempting to pull him down to her.

He didn't budge, just gently unlatched her arms and set her away from him.

Her eyes shot to his, no doubt filled with the question pinging around in her mind. Why was he stopping? She could feel his arousal across the bond. It blazed as hot as her own.

His lips turned up. "Because if we don't stop now. I'm going to have you sprawled across that bed." He crouched a little, a slight stoop that put their stares at equal level. "And as much as I want *that*, pleasuring you within an inch of your life isn't exactly taking things slow."

"But I want you," she said then frowned at the almost whining tone. "Never mind. I don't want to be that girl." Feeling slightly stung and knowing with absolute certainty that she had no reason to, she began to turn away.

He stopped her with a hand on her arm. "I want you," he said, rotating her so that she faced him fully.

"I know," she said. His desire still reigned firm along their link, still made her quiver with need. But beneath that passion was reticence, and the connection they shared wasn't strong enough for her to discern whether that was because he didn't *want* to want her—if that even made sense—or if it really was his intention to take things slow that had him throwing up the red light.

The curse that flew from his lips startled her.

She jumped. "Wh-wh—?" she stammered, not even getting the entire question out before his mouth slammed onto hers.

This time there was more than just his lips. The kiss was teeth and tongue, hands and body. His presence threatened to overwhelm her, it was so damned strong but, despite her inexperience, she wasn't scared. More like every nerve in her body was finally functioning, finally firing. She finally felt alive.

Reaching down, he swept her into his arms and carried her into her bedroom.

Like all of the single Rengalla, her quarters were the equivalent of a studio apartment.

The short hallway opened into a large room that was bigger than the trailer she'd spent her entire childhood in. The bed was centered between two doors, one that led to a large walk-in closet and the other that opened up into a spa-like bathroom, complete with marble counter tops and antique bronze fixtures.

It was the nicest place she'd ever lived, and her sparse belongings looked ridiculous amongst the opulent furnishings.

But Mason didn't spare any of that a second glance.

He strode across the room with her in his arms, tossed her on the bed, and followed her down onto the mattress.

Everywhere. He was absolutely *everywhere*.

His hands and mouth worked in tandem. It was both overwhelming and damned good at the same time. Slightly calloused fingers traced down her cheeks, her neck, along the sides of her breasts to her waist. They slipped underneath her T-shirt and slid slowly—*too slowly*—back up. Each lackadaisical circle brought his hands closer to the place she wanted him, only to have him stop just shy of her bra.

Before she could complain, before she could rip her mouth away from his and demand that he give her what she wanted, Mason reached beneath her and unhooked the clasp of her bra.

Pushing it and her shirt up, his mouth lasered in on her aching nipple. He took one hard pull that had her gasping and grabbing his head to hold him closer at the same time.

"*Mason*," she moaned as he used his teeth and tongue, sending desire scorching through her body, making her pussy ache, her thighs clench together.

He switched to the other side. "I love it when you say my name."

Her response was lost when he gave her other nipple the same determined attention. Hips tilting in unfulfilled need, she writhed against him, her body instinctively seeking more, *needing* more. Thankfully, he gave it to her, his hand sliding down and unclasping her jeans, and slipped work-roughened fingers beneath the elastic of her underwear arrowing straight for the spot she *needed* to be touched. He circled her clit, pressed firmly, and . . . it took less than two minutes before she was shouting his name and flying over the cliff.

When she came back to earth, he withdrew his hand and buttoned her jeans then rolled to his side and pulled her close. Her ponytail had come loose and the strands itched her face. He brushed them back, running his fingers through the slightly tangled locks. After a moment, he chuckled softly. "I don't think I ever understood the meaning of bases until right now."

"Hmm?" she asked, feeling too sated to care much about what he was saying. And though she figured she should probably offer to reciprocate the favor, she needed to regain the feeling in her limbs in order to do so.

Give her five minutes.

"I think I just made it to third base."

Finally comprehending what he was saying, she laughed. "Proud of yourself, are you?"

"Mmhmm," he murmured, brushing a kiss to the top of her head. "I also don't think I've ever necked like a teenager either."

She cuddled into his chest. "Necked?" she teased. "You're showing your age, old man."

He ran a hand down her spine. "Maybe," he said. It froze mid-journey as hesitation slunk into the connection of their minds. "I didn't scare you did I? I was too . . . focused on—" His breath caught. "After everything that happened to you, I don't want you to not feel in control."

Affection for the man lying next to her made her heart swell almost to the point of bursting. "I'm not scared." She waffled for a moment, trying to decide how to tell him. In the end, she just blurted it out. "I'm a virgin. Not because I necessarily want to be, but . . ." She sighed. "I didn't—I didn't even know about *Netflix* until I came here. My opportunities were—" She broke off, her cheeks hot and she had to force herself to hold his stare.

Silence stretched until finally he spoke, the words careful.

Soft. "It doesn't matter to me if you're not." A beat. "Whether you chose to, or were forced. I wouldn't care."

A burst of irritation slid through her, and she sat up, pulling her shirt down and crossing her arms. "Look, I'm a virgin, okay? I'm twenty-seven years old and haven't had sex." She threw up her hands. "That's just the reality." She sighed. "And I told you before . . . those men kissed me, touched me, *cornered* me, but they didn't—" A shake of her head. "I was able to stop it from going further."

Chagrin softened the hard planes of his face and he pushed himself up to sit next to her. "I didn't mean it to sound as though I didn't believe you." He faltered for a moment and Gabby swore that his cheeks went a little pink. "I just . . . I never understood why men thought they were allowed to put value on what a woman did with her body, or didn't do, or had no control over." He ran his fingers lightly down her throat. "And it wouldn't matter to me because what's important is us. *Now*."

Her lips parted, a response on the tip of her tongue when there was a pounding knock on the door.

She gasped at the same time that Mason cursed.

"Fifteen minutes and counting until dinner, bro!" a voice Gabby recognized as one of Mason's brothers—but not which one—hollered. "Better get your ass in gear unless you want Mom storming down here!"

With another curse, Mason grabbed her hand and pulled her to her feet.

"You'd better get changed," he said with a light smack to her bottom and a push in the direction of the bathroom. "He's not jokine about her storming down here."

TWENTY-SIX

Mason

HE WALKED alongside Gabby down the hall to his mother's rooms.

Her cheeks were still flushed from the orgasm and blonde tendrils escaped from her ponytail. Unfortunately she was also dressed, but that was probably for the best. The sight of her naked breasts, of the curve of her hips, the soft moans she made as she came—

Damn.

The urge to skip dinner, to keep her in that bed until she was lax and sated and—

So not helping his problem.

Concentrating on trying to get blood to flow away from his groin instead of to it, he turned his focus to the murals coating the walls. The colorful, three-dimensional images depicted everything from pounding waves to abstract Pollack-like renderings were easy to get lost in. They were the batteries of the Colony, siphoning off extra magic, fueling everything from the heating and air conditioning to the lights overhead.

Including, his mother's kitchen.

He knew she'd be working overtime, cooking all of their favorites, and it felt odd to be going to a family dinner with someone. He hadn't brought home a woman since Victoria. Not that he'd brought her home, exactly. More like they'd been properly introduced at the right balls and parties, a product of a more formal time.

Things had changed. Years had passed.

And . . . Gabby was different.

They were still learning each other, but he already cared about her deeply, and more importantly . . . he didn't want to screw things up.

Even as that thought entered his mind, she squeezed his fingers. The touch was soft, almost gentle, and he felt her consciousness sweep against his own.

"There you go again," she murmured.

"It's nothing." But he knew he needed to get his shit together if he didn't want to fuck up the single good thing in his life since Victoria. Which was the problem, wasn't it? His fear that Gabby would be taken from him in the same way, his desperate desire to protect her, the gnawing terror he would fail.

"It's *not* nothing," she said, coming closer, brushing her shoulder against his. "But considering that we're about to meet your mother, I'll give you a free pass this one time."

His mouth twitched, but the impact on his soul was huge. He could almost feel the tethers strengthening, tying him even more firmly to her.

Quite simply, she was incredible.

She'd been through hell, and she was . . . perfect.

Her eyes locked onto his. "However," she said with a series of intense finger gestures between the pair of them. "We *will* talk about this soon."

The dark emotions were swept away by a sudden mischievousness that made him feel about a hundred years younger. Going with it, he leaned close enough to whisper in her ear, her citrus scent surrounding him, intoxicating him. "Do I get a reprieve if I promise you more orgasms?"

Her lips parted, heat tinged her cheeks, and her pulse was rapid beneath the skin of her throat. Then she shuddered and stepped back. "You're dangerous."

"Don't I know it," he murmured, but instead of allowing the poisonous fears to creep back into his mind, he determinedly pushed them away.

"What's your mother like?" she asked as they turned a corner into yet another hall.

The Colony was a beehive of interconnected hallways and corridors set in Northern Kentucky. It was isolated and on easily defendable grounds—surrounded by lakes on two sides, the forest on the other, the waterfalls on the last—and the terrain was both hidden and sheltered. So, despite his idiotic campout beyond Daughtry and Cody's bond-magic-fueled shield, it was more secure than ever before. If some unsuspecting human did manage to make their way through the vast waterways or find the carefully obscured—by earth magic—forest road, the building they found at the road's end was glamoured to be as ugly and abandoned-looking as possible. No sane mortal would approach.

Of course, it didn't appear that way to the Rengalla. For the people who lived here, the surroundings were filled with marble and crystal, real hardwood floors and the murals lining the walls.

And his mother was the woman who had designed it all.

The glamours that hid them from prying mortal eyes, and everything else—from color schemes to throw pillows for the entire Colony. She had an entire team beneath that worked with implementing her ideas and upkeep and any changes that needed to be made. A different team—Mason was their liaison from the security side—made sure the Colony had the most technologically advanced equipment available. Anyone who lived at the Colony, worked for Rengallan businesses, or soldiered were taken care of—and they all shared in the profits equally.

The good thing about having living for centuries was that long-term investments took on a whole new meaning.

Of course, there were those like Gabby's family who chose not to live or work for the Rengalla, to strike out on their own. They were free to do so, and it was John and his team's responsibility being to try and make sure they didn't slip through the cracks.

A difficult job, especially when keeping ties over many decades.

People tended to grow apart over time, and the Rengalla had been no different. Millennia had caused fractures and long lives also had long memories. But as their fight against the Dalshie had intensified, most had preferred to live at the Colony or another Rengallan establishment—they had several around the world. The fight was brutal and soul-crushing, but in a way it had been the best thing for their people, rebuilding connections, strengthening ties, and ultimately to help bolstering their businesses and the strategies they had in place to protect their people.

They were in a much better place today than a century before.

But they still had a fuck-ton of work to do.

"Mason?"

Gabby's voice had him blinking out of his mental reverie and replaying their conversation so he could answer her. "My mother is great."

She glanced over at him and he didn't need to hear her say, "Seriously?" He'd heard it loud and clear along the bond.

Her irritation made him chuckle. "I was getting to the rest of it," he said, tugging a strand of her hair. "She's a designer." He made a gesture that encompassed the walls around them. "Was the one who decorated the Colony, in fact."

"She did all of this?" Gabby asked, incredulous. "It's beautiful." She winced as they passed a mural that looked more like magical upchuck than actual. "Well . . . some of the murals are a little hit or miss. But the furnishings, the colors are gorgeous."

"She'll appreciate that," he said with a smile. "It was a bit of a struggle to get some of the former Council to okay the changes."

What used to be the ruling arm of the Rengalla had recently been dismantled, and Mason, for one, approved. Their people didn't need bureaucracy. They needed good leadership—those who looked to the future, watched out for their vulnerable, built up their defenses and businesses so that they would *have* a future.

"Really?" Gabby asked. "But it's beautiful and classic and—"

He rolled his eyes. "They had a hard time parting with the columns and gold leaf and busy wallpaper of Europe. They didn't like her scaled-down approach."

"*This* is *scaled-down*?" Gabby's eyes were wide as she glanced around. "There's more marble in this place than a museum." She tapped her knuckles against the wooden wainscoting. "I don't think there's one thing in this entire place that isn't custom made, from the cabinets in my room to this trim."

"That's probably true." His lips twitch. "I do remember her mentioning a few years ago when they were redoing everything that there were too much Earth magic specialists with too little to do and she was going to give them something to fill their time."

"How'd that work?"

"She got them growing trees." A beat. "After the first lot, she found they were really busy with other things."

Gabby grinned. "I bet they did."

"Good news," he said, "is we got the Gardens out of it, and they were much happier not seeing the products of their hard work going into a mill."

"Win-win."

He snaked an arm around her waist. "For everyone, including Mom, who also got her landscaping vision realized."

She snorted. "I think I love her."

"Most people do," he said. "She's a big personality, but she had to be to put up with Monroe, Morgan, and I."

A sigh. "I can't believe I'm dating a triplet. It seems like something out of those bad reality shows Dee forces me to watch."

"Dee forces you?" He fixed her in place with a stare, felt the blip of her guilt in his mind. "You mean to tell me you don't enjoy watching librarians yell at each other? Or criticizing wedding dresses?"

"Nope." A sigh. "They force me. The burden is a terrible one."

Laughing, loving the amusement, the happiness he could sense in her mind, he directed her to the right at the next corner.

His mother's quarters were just ahead, a large suite of rooms she'd offered to give up after he and his brothers had moved out, but one she'd been encouraged to keep nonetheless. She had more visitors and meetings than most of the other Rengalla, and the extra space had been put to good use. Plus, she had her own kitchen in the suite, and as much as everyone loved the food the cooks prepared, no one was shy about dropping in for a meal when his mother was cooking.

His mouth was already watering.

"I like that one," Gabby murmured, slowing by a mural that depicted a barren mountaintop covered with snow. "It's stark, but beautiful."

"Does it remind you of home?" he asked, curious.

She was quiet for a few moments. "Yes, I didn't think about that, but in a way, it is like my childhood. Dark and dangerous, but with moments of such piercing beauty that the hazards could almost be forgotten." Her ponytail bobbed as she shook her head. "Ugh. That sounds ridiculous."

"No," he said, halting her when she would have started walking again. "It's not stupid. It's beautiful. And true." He sent his mind along their link, urging her to feel his sincerity. "Life is like that, right? We're lulled into easy comforts, we forget to give thanks for the things we have, and then everything can be shattered, torn away with something as senseless as an avalanche."

He held those pretty brown eyes until she nodded, until her breath shuddered out. "Yes," she murmured, turning toward him and lightly cupping his jaw. "You're right."

Resisting the urge to kiss her, to make them both forget about the past, he tugged her forward.

They walked in silence, but wasn't uncomfortable, nor was it the amiable silence of friends or lovers. Their minds were filled with memories of their pasts, of hopes for their future. And in that moment, he knew everything that held him back—his fears, his failures—was meaningless. This woman was more important than *all* of those things.

Because . . . holy fucking shit, he loved her.

Somehow, she'd become his heartbeat, woven so deeply that she was in the very marrow of his bones, and he couldn't give that up, couldn't give up the chance at a future with her—not for any cost.

He was enough. He *had* to be enough.

For Victoria and Daniel. For Gabby. For himself.

He couldn't retreat and keep living cut off from the world. He wanted to live. He wanted to spend his life loving this woman, helping her through the darkness, and hopefully one day earning her love back.

His heart pounded, but if Gabby sensed the trend of his thoughts, she didn't show it. He felt as though he'd been rocked by a nuke and she was walking along peacefully oblivious.

Was this how Cody had felt?

That his every cell belonged to Daughtry, that he would do *anything* to see her smile?

It was unnerving, it was overwhelming, and . . . he wanted more.

He wanted all of her.

His magic tickled his mind, urging him to let it loose, to complete the bonding. He held back only because he'd promised he would. But the moment she was ready, he would solidify the connection between them, would link their souls permanently.

Calm settled over him at the thought.

He'd made his decision. He wouldn't let the past destroy it.

Signed. Sealed. Delivered.

"So natural triplets, huh?" she asked, tugging him out of his own thoughts. "A couple hundred years ago, that must have been a risky pregnancy."

"So I've heard," he grumbled. "Only about a million times." He flashed her a quick grin when she laughed, showing her he was kidding. Slightly. "But the healers helped my mother through the entire, apparently arduous, nine months."

Her laugh was music to his soul, lightening him until he was almost buoyant with happiness.

"Is your dad still . . . ?"

He grimaced, but the memories couldn't completely darken his mood. "No. The Dalshie killed my father in their attacks during WWII."

"I'm sorry." She leaned her head against his shoulder. "I didn't know."

He shrugged. "It was a long time ago, and I've been able to come to terms."

"But your wife, your son, your father." Her voice was grim. "You have so much cause to hate them." The volume dropped so that it was almost inaudible. "You should hate *me* for loving—"

He stopped and wrapped her in his arms. "Trust me when I say that I could never hate you, Sunshine."

"Er-hem."

His gaze flew up, saw his mother standing in the doorway to her quarters. Rolling his eyes, he released Gabby, snagged her hand, and led her toward his mother.

He would bide his time, would woo her, would show her that he loved her.

And when she finally trusted him with every bit of her soul, he would bond with her, take that final step to permanently claim her as his.

Because she was his, as much as he would be forever hers.

TWENTY-SEVEN

Gabby

SHE STOOD DUMBSTRUCK in the hall, staring at the woman Mason had introduced as his mother in utter disbelief.

"It's true, I'm afraid," Matilda said, her lips twitching. "I somehow carried those three boys to term."

Her smile was kind, and there was amusement in her hazel eyes, in the single most striking feature that connected her with her sons. Add in similar hair color—both brown but not the same shade—and perhaps, there was something in their bone structure that linked them, but . . . the biggest difference was in size.

It wasn't that she had expected Mason's mother to be six feet tall like her sons, but she hadn't expected the petite woman —several inches shorter than Gabby's own five feet practically nothing—to be so small.

Triplets?

Matilda laughed. "Yup," she said. "All three of them." A beat. "At the same time."

Gabby felt her face flush. Was Mason's mother telepathic?

"No," Matilda said. "I'm not telepathic and can't read emotions. I've just had these questions multiple times over the last two centuries, sweetie."

"Oh, I'm sorry," she said, embarrassed. "It's frankly"—she shook her head, laughed—"impressive."

"I like you already," Matilda said, leaning in for a quick hug.

Gabby froze, instincts she'd forgotten she possessed after being so long in Mason's presence, rearing their ugly heads. It took her a moment to get used to the strange set of arms, to force the automatic reaction away, and hug Matilda back.

Mason's mother released her. "I'm sorry," she said. "I'm a hugger." An awkward pause punctuated the air. "Sometimes I forget that not everyone is."

"It's not that," she said, surprising herself. "I didn't mind it." A shrug, discomfort making the movement jerky. "I'm . . ." Her gaze dropped to the floor, her voice dropping alongside it. "I'm just not used to it."

It was the simplest truth without exposing her sordid past to Mason's mother.

Though it was probably pointless, she realized when she managed to look up again and saw Matilda staring at her with a considering expression on her face. One that said she'd seen right through Gabby's glossing over of the details.

"Mom," Mason said, gently touching Gabby's arm and carefully inserting himself between the two women. "I'm hungry."

Matilda laughed. "Oh, my favorite oldest triplet, you always are. Come on in, dinner's ready." She stepped back from the door and waved them in. "Make yourselves comfortable. I'll just set the table then holler when it's ready."

Mason led her down the hall, and she saw that Matilda's quarters were much larger than Gabby's. She had an actual entryway, decorated with an elegant circular table and a gilded mirror, and from there another short hallway opened up into a large living space.

This was no studio apartment.

The room was soft, airy, and filled with equally delicate furniture—a couch and loveseat, tables, even a row of bookcases adorned one wall. A small pass-through afforded her a view of Matilda in the kitchen and opposite them was a small, well-appointed dining room.

While Gabby was struck by the elegance of her surroundings, Mason was unfazed. He pulled her toward the couch and plunked down, tucking her right against his side.

"This is gorgeous," she murmured.

Mason just shrugged. "My mom is talented."

"Uh. Yeah." Everything in the space was at once comfortable and suave, stunning and yet not stuffy, the perfect mix of hotel chic and lived-in.

Talented didn't begin to cover the breadth of Matilda's abilities.

She opened her mouth to ask him what it had been like to grow up in such a place, but his groan of displeasure stifled her words. He shifted away from her, slid his hand behind a pillow.

"What is it?" she asked.

He winced. "Nothing."

But there was something about the quick response, the way he held himself, the angle of his body as he shielded—

After taking a quick mental stock, gauging where his mind was at, making sure the blip of emotion she felt in his consciousness wasn't serious, she grinned. Nope, definitely not serious. Rather, he was embarrassed.

"What are you hiding?" she asked, trying to reach around him.

"Nothing."

Another rapid reply and a giggle passed through her lips because the expression on his face—little boy who'd gotten caught with his hand in the cookie jar—was so unlike him.

"Let me see." She reached forward.

He moved back. "There's nothing to see here."

"I'd call B.S. on that," she said, attempting to wriggle past him.

His arms closed around her and he hauled her into his lap.

"Mason!" she gasped, glancing over her shoulder, half expecting Matilda to walk in and find Gabby crawling all over her son. Squirming, she attempted to extract herself, but his arms may as well have been steel for all the effect she had on them. "Let me go!"

He leaned down, nipped her ear. "Keep moving like that and I'm not going to be able to stand up."

"Wh-what?" she asked, then shifted again and stifled a groan, biting her lip in desire, in laughter as she comprehended —or rather, *felt* what he meant. He was hard, his arms not the only body part that resembled steel.

"Do you feel what you do to me?" His question was rasped, ratcheting her arousal up to a seriously-inappropriate-for-visiting-his-mother level.

She needed to calm things down, so instead of admitting that his hard cock between her thighs made her ache for him, she kept her tone light. "This is starting to become a problem for you," she murmured, pressing a quick kiss to his lips.

But when he tried to deepen the contact, she tickled his side and grabbed for the object he'd been attempting to hide.

As soon as her fingers grasped the bound book, she scrambled off his lap and into the armchair on the opposite side of the coffee table.

He growled, started to follow, when Matilda strode back into the room. "The roast just needs another few—Oh good! You found it."

Reeling, her gaze jumping from Mason's scorching expression to Matilda's placid kindness, Gabby fumbled with the book. "Um . . . yes?"

"This is my favorite part." Matilda clapped her hands together gleefully. "The point where I get to embarrass my kids. Photos are traditional, are they not?"

Gabby frowned. "But they didn't have photos when Mason was a baby."

"No," Matilda said. "But they did have these."

She flipped the cover open, and Gabby felt her jaw drop open.

The images inside were similar to the murals that lined the hallway, though miniature and instead of landscapes they were of Mason and his brothers. As babies, as toddlers, and older—on horses, in a tree, in fancy old-fashioned suit, even holding a rifle.

Good lord, even as a gangly teenager he had still been gorgeous.

Of course *he'd* skip the awkward stage.

As her fingers began to turn the page, Mason's hand halted her. She looked up, surprised she hadn't sensed him come over. "That's far enough," he said, sitting on the arm of her chair.

"What—?" she started to ask then caught the trail of his thoughts.

The next pages were of him and Victoria and Jacob.

She paused as she considered her feelings. She wasn't jealous of Victoria, more curious. But did that curiosity mean she should bring up the painful parts of Mason's past?

No.

Gently closing the book, she set it aside and turned to him, cupping his cheek. "When you're ready to show me, I would like to see them," she murmured.

"Sunshine," he whispered, his voice gruff, and she felt him brace. "You can look if you want."

"Some other time." She quickly pressed her lips to his. "When it's not quite so raw."

His breath caught, the pulse of emotion he sent down their connection warming her from the inside out, but before she could say anything further, a slight rustling sound drew her attention and she turned, surprised and a little uncomfortable that she'd so easily forgotten the presence of Mason's mother.

Matilda had the oddest expression on her face—amazement and concern, affection and approval.

That affection, the approval.

Her breath caught. So freely and easily given.

Why had her own mother been incapable of providing it? Why had she been unable to love an innocent little girl? She knew she might never understand her mother's motivations, but for the first time Gabby actually believed that she'd had no bearing on them whatsoever.

Mason had said it wasn't her fault.

John, Dante, Dee, and Suz hadn't treated her like a victim, exactly—probably because they didn't have all of the details—but they *had* acknowledged that Gabby wasn't to blame.

And yet part of her had never truly believed *any* of them.

Funny how the course of a person's life could change with a simple look. That all of the pieces could realign in response to a fleeting glance.

It wasn't her fault.

It. Wasn't. Her. Fault.

"May I use the bathroom?" she asked, surprised at how outwardly calm she sounded.

Matilda's face cleared. "Of course. It's the second door on the right."

Rising, she nodded then walked down the hall. She felt rather than heard Mason stand to follow her.

"I'm okay," she thought.

He blinked at the sound of her mental voice then, *"I'm not so sure."*

Gabby blinked herself, hearing him across their connection. It surprised her how clear it sounded, and also how intimate it felt, as though his voice was flowing across her soul.

Almost *too* intimate.

Deep inside, how did he feel about her? Did she want to know?

"You can look if you want," he thought. *"I don't have anything to hide from you, Sunshine."*

She almost smiled at the placating tone of his mind. They might share a growing mental link, but it didn't ensure clarity. He could feel her emotions, understand that something had rocked her to the core, and yet he had no clue that the emotions coursing through her—the ones making her heart pound, her hands tremble, her throat tight as hell—weren't any fault of his.

"I don't need to look," she thought. *"I just need a minute."* With that, she walked to the bathroom, gently closed the door behind her, and leaned against it.

Why had she spent so long blaming herself?

It seemed ridiculous as she looked back on the events of her childhood. The memories weren't pleasant—rather, they were mostly terrible. And somehow, she'd taken that upon herself, *blamed* herself for having affection to the woman who birthed who, who occasionally showed her kindness.

And hating her, as well.

Because the good times had made Gabby accept the bad.

Why? Perhaps, she had a flaw in her character, something that made her vulnerable to mistreatment.

Bullshit.

Yes, that was *all* bullshit. She loved her father—that was easy to quantify—and she loved the good parts of her mother—that was the way forward. Resting her head back against the cool wood, she bent her knees and slid to the floor. She supposed the way she categorized her conflicted feelings didn't really matter, so long as she stopped shouldering the blame for what had happened.

Easier said than done. But progress wasn't always a steady track and she—

The knock on the door made her jump.

It was Mason. She knew that before he even spoke.

"Let me in, Sunshine."

"I'm fine," she called. "Just . . . give me a minute." She stood, crossed to the sink, and splashed some water on her face, thankful she hadn't had time to fuss with makeup. She was still learning how to put it on, and in this instance, she was glad she could wash her face and didn't have to deal with racoon eyes. And maybe it was the inane thoughts of makeup, or the noise of the running water, or perhaps it was simply the swirling emotions in her mind, but regardless, she didn't realize that Mason had ignored her and entered the bathroom anyway until she was in his arms.

"What—?" she asked, not having a chance to finish the question before his lips pressed against hers.

It was a hard kiss, a firm meeting of their mouths, his grip on her waist no less resolved.

"Tell me," he demanded when he'd pulled back slightly, the puffs of his breath teasing her lips, his arms stiff bands around her.

She shook her head, a weak attempt to clear her mind. "Tell you what?"

Scowling, he gently touched the corner of one eye. "Tell me why you've been crying."

"I'm not!" She'd held back the tears.

Mason made a sound of disapproval. "I can feel you, you know that, right? There's no point in lying. And besides that, your nose is red, your eyes are watery, and your cheeks are flushed."

"I didn't cry," she muttered then at his disbelieving scoff added, "So maybe I came close, but it was out of happiness. I wasn't upset."

"The turmoil I sensed in your mind wasn't happiness."

"I didn't say it was *all* happiness." She shoved at his arms, but he didn't release her. "I just said I *was* happy." Struggling in earnest now, frustrated that he could hold her when she wanted some distance to align her thoughts, she snapped, "Let me go."

He shook his head. "Spill."

"Why do you—?" A grunt escaped as her elbow connected with his stomach. "Why do you get to keep all of your confidences and I have to give you every detail? There are things I've wanted to demand of you, but I haven't because I respect that you deserve privacy to work things out in your mind. Why can't you do that for me?"

It was almost comical how quickly his arms dropped. And then how quickly they rose again to steady her when she stumbled from their sudden loss.

"I don't know."

The three words were soft and filled with such dismay that Gabby forgot she was frustrated and closed the distance between them this time.

"No." She sighed. "Don't start shouldering that blame." She ran her fingers across his jaw, tried to get him to meet her eyes.

"Let's just stop and start over. I don't expect you to give me everything—every thought and insight that flicks through your mind." Another sigh as he continued to stare over her head. "We're new at this. I'm okay with taking it slow. So long as you don't go all alpha and try to get me to spill every detail, but you keep all the hurts and pain inside. I can't be with someone who does that." She touched his jaw. "*We* can't work like that."

His shoulders rose and dropped on one long breath. "You're right. I'm sorry."

Her heart pulse, but she kept her tone light. "Was that as painful to say as it sounded?"

His chuckle was a little forced, but at least he looked at her. "Sorry I pushed."

"I want this to work," she said, "so I'm not going to say it's okay. Because it's not, and I'm done with letting people hurt me. But . . . I know the bond is playing with our emotions, making us both a little crazy." She smiled. "But we also need to have some privacy, right?"

"Right." He grimaced. "I just . . . I don't want ignore something, pretend a problem doesn't exist and then have it fester between us."

She nodded because he had a point. "How about I promise to tell you if it's important?"

"Who decides it's important?"

"I do." She touched the frown that appeared. "And you have to trust that I won't lie to you about it."

Hazel eyes on hers, holding for a long moment. Then a slight incline of his head. "Okay, Sunshine. I'm good with that."

"And you'll do the same?"

His hopeful demeanor dimmed slightly, and she felt his mind grow serious as he considered whether or not that was something he could do. After a moment, he nodded. "Yes."

"Okay then," she said. "Is this the point where I should tell you that I've finally stopped blaming myself for my past?" Rising on tiptoe, she pressed a quick kiss to his mouth and leaned in to whisper in his ear. "Is that important enough for you?"

Leaving Mason appearing as though he'd been struck across the face with a two by four, she walked out of the bathroom and back toward the living space.

Her stomach growled, abruptly ravenous. Time for dinner.

TWENTY-EIGHT

Mason

HE STARED at Gabby across his mother's dinner table no doubt looking like the most besotted idiot of all time.

She'd dropped a bomb just before she'd strode out of the bathroom—saying that the past no longer had a hold on her.

Just like that.

Shaking his head in amazement, he continued shoving food into his mouth and listened as his mother gave Gabby the fifth degree. He knew he should intervene, despite the fact that he was still reeling from the revelation, but when he concentrated on the bond, focused on Gabby's mind, she wasn't distraught like before.

No. She was content, even happy with the attention.

Until his mother asked, "And your parents, Gabby? Where are they?"

Silence blossomed in the room, filled the space between them with an almost tangible tension.

But before he could say anything, Gabby straightened her shoulders. "My parents are dead," she answered softly.

"Oh. I'm sorry, sweetie."

"Thank you." Gabby took a bite of her meal then he felt her close the door in her mind, doing what she'd declared in the bathroom and leaving her past behind "You have to tell me how you made these, Matilda. I swear I could live on mashed potatoes alone."

Just like that, Mason thought.

Just like that Gabby had shed the mantle of the past and focused on the future.

He wondered if he'd be able to do the same.

He was exhausted. He'd been scouring the monitors, scheduling extra patrols, and was just coming off his own twelve-hour watch.

His body ached. His mind was spent. And he desperately wanted to see Gabby.

Which was going to have to wait.

Unless he planned on knocking her straight into unconsciousness with his stink, the first thing he *had* to do was take a shower. After that he planned to swoop in, steal her from the infirmary, and feed her. If he'd learned anything about her over the last two weeks—two weeks in which he'd spent every spare moment with Gabby, two weeks that had left his body hard and aching, his soul craving even more contact with her—it was that she didn't put her own well-being above others.

Which meant that if Suz pulled crazy hours in the clinic, Gabby stayed too. If Daughtry needed help restocking supplies or, hell, for Gabby to *do* the restocking because Cody had spirited Daughtry away, then Gabby did it.

So now he was going to do his part in taking care of *his* bondmate.

A blip in his mind signified that Gabby knew he'd arrived back inside. *"I'll shower and be there in fifteen,"* he thought to her. *"I hope you're ready for me."*

They were too far for full telepathic communication without the bond being fully invoked, but he could feel that she'd understood, if not every word, then at least his intention.

Walking briskly, he made it to his quarters and was in the shower in record time.

His thoughts traveled between Gabby and the Dalshie at the waterfalls. There had been no further sign of their presence outside the shield—neither the cameras nor the increased patrols discovered anything.

A rogue attack.

Which wasn't exceptionally unusual—they'd volleyed strikes on the Rengallan stronghold after Daughtry had come to live there. That was why the shield was so important and why civilian Rengalla were not allowed outside of it.

But . . . there hadn't been an attack in months, not since Daughtry had killed the person who'd been masterminding the attacks.

The Dalshie's reappearance now, after all this time, was concerning.

So were those Dalshie merely been remnants leftover from the previous battle? Or was there more at hand? Was another attack forthcoming?

Turning up the hot water, he allowed it to sluice over his head and down his back, letting the worries about the Dalshie fall away. He wouldn't find the answers in the shower, and he wasn't the only one fighting, wouldn't have to shoulder the burden alone.

Instead, his attention returned to Gabby—a much more pleasant avenue with which to lose his thoughts.

So young, so sweet and innocent that he almost couldn't

believe the things she'd been through. Not that she was weak—not at all, he'd never had a woman call him on his shit more—but she had an intrinsic *sunniness* that made him feel a hundred years younger.

And any traced of hesitation, of tentativeness in her dealings with him had disappeared after that declaration in the bathroom.

She'd made a choice . . . and she was following through.

God, it was impossible how much he loved the woman.

He reached up and cranked off the water, the urge to see her rising within him, ratcheting his need to nearly stifling levels. It had been a long two weeks.

Patience.

Right. Sighing, he stepped out of the shower, snagged a towel off the hook then dried himself and tied it around his waist. Snagging another to dry his hair, he left the bathroom.

The need to complete the bond was a bone deep ache, and he physically hurt with keeping his desire in check. He *wanted* her, so fucking badly—

His feet skidded to a stop in what was probably a comical reaction.

The towel he'd been using on his hair dropped to the carpet.

Because he wasn't alone.

Gabby lay beneath the covers of his bed.

Pale brown eyes met his own and she smiled, an intoxicating mix of sweet and sexy as hell.

"What are you doing?" he asked, his voice going past roughened and straight to gravel.

Hands came up to grasp the comforter to her chest and she sat up. "I missed you," she murmured. Her petite shoulders were bare, and his cock hardened when he caught a glimpse of her clothes folded neatly in the chair in the corner. "I needed to see you."

"Naked?" His feet carried him across the room before his mind even registered the action.

Her smile went a little wicked. "Not *quite* naked." And though her grip on the comforter was so tight that the bones of her fingers pressed against her skin, though he could feel her mind was full of nerves, she took a breath and tossed the blanket aside.

Mason cursed, slammed his eyes shut, and tried to breath.

"I'm ready, baby," she murmured.

"No," he said. "I don't want to rush—"

Hands on his cheeks. "But *I* want." A beat of hesitation. "Unless, you think—"

He kissed her, thinking that he needed something more than the towel around his waist, if he was going to make this last. The temptation to drop the slip of cotton and plunge inside her was so great that his hands actually ached from resisting. Especially, when he pulled back and opened his eyes again, and saw what she was wearing.

Her curves were clad in the sexiest scraps of lace he'd ever seen in his life.

A strapless bra on top, tiny panties on the bottom. Both were black and see-through, doing nothing to hide the rosy peaks of her breasts, the blond hair between her legs. The bra was skimpy, so small that if she breathed wrong, a nipple might pop out.

He found himself pleading for that to be the case.

He hadn't touched Gabby since that day two week ago—well, nothing more than kisses and hugs and the careful stroke of her curves. Because as more time went on, the desperate urge to take increased, and he didn't to devour and mark her sun-kissed skin until she was ready.

"I like the lace."

Warmth down their connection, affection in her eyes. "I'm glad, honey," she whispered.

Love. So much love for her. So much need and desire, enough to make his head spin. But he gritted his teeth, breathed through it. Because if this was to be her first time, he was going to make it good.

His eyes drifted from her face, to her breasts, mouth watering to taste, then down further to the tiny piece of lace that was supposed to be her panties. Where to start? Where to—

"Mason?"

"Hmm?" he asked, knowing he was staring and yet completely unable to stop. Her hips were curvy, her breasts bountiful, her legs long and lean.

"Are you only going to look?" Her voice shook slightly and when he studied her face he saw the mix of amusement and uncertainty within her expression.

"You are so damned beautiful," he whispered.

He closed the distance between them, pulled her into his arms, and kissed her. She opened immediately, her tongue brushing against his. Only when his lungs screamed for air, did he break free. Gabby reached for him again, attempted to twine her arms around his neck, but he snagged them and held her still.

Praying for a modicum of restraint, he gazed into her eyes. They were glazed with desire and her hips, free to move, undulated in a maddening rhythm against his own.

But he had to ask. *Had* to be certain before he got in too deep.

So he grasped on to the last dredges of his sanity and asked, "Are you sure?"

TWENTY-NINE

Gabby

SHE FROZE at his rough question.

She felt crazed, every inch of her body on fire. But the open concern in his expression, the seriousness of his mind against hers gave her enough clarity that she paused.

Was she sure?

A heartbeat of time was all it took. "Yes."

He shuddered, his forehead dropping to her collarbone, his breath hot on her skin. Then he lifted his head, his eyes meeting hers. "I love you, Sunshine. I never thought I would be able to feel this way again, never thought I could feel this *much*."

"I—"

He lifted a hand and touched a finger to her lips. "Let me say this?" At her nod, he continued. "I was hiding when I met you. Scared to be hurt, as pathetic as that is. But you have this spine of steel. You're so impossibly sweet and strong, and . . . you gave me the courage to feel." Moving his finger, he brushed back the hair from her face. "You're inside of me, straight down to my DNA. In my soul, my heart, and I love you."

Every nerve in her body focused in rigid attention. She'd expected some compliments, maybe an endearment or two, but this was so much more. He'd bared himself, sliced out his heart, and handed it to her.

Did she dare take it?

How could she not?

And how could she not lay out her own offering in return?

She tugged at her arms, still held in his firm grasp. "Let me go."

He released her, caution filling his eyes, and slowly, so that he understood she was one hundred percent cognizant of her actions, she reached up and grasped his face in both of her hands.

"You need to know," she whispered and when his body tensed, she pressed on, "I love you, too."

A shuddering breath passed through his lips. "You do?"

She nodded. "I do."

His arms banded around her hips and pulled her close, holding her tight. His heart pounded against hers, his breathing was unsteady. She loved this man so much, had found the person who felt like the other half of her soul.

But instead of saying any of that, she simply . . . released the hold on her magic.

It was easy.

Her powers *wanted* to mesh with his, had been pushing her to be connected with Mason's every moment she spent with him, so the release happened quickly. Pale brown magic crawled down her spine and out her palms. It balled there, waiting for him to follow suit.

"Gab—"

He froze, eyes wide. Then he moved abruptly, the motions jerky, the flow of his magic sudden and intense—strands of green and gold and brown interwove with her own.

Holy hell.

She'd never felt anything so good. It was absolute ecstasy. It was a hairsbreadth shy of being too intense. It was—

His mouth slammed down onto hers and she lost track of any thoughts, of anything aside from the feel of his lips against hers, of his hard body, of the firm grip he had on her waist.

Strands of green and pale brown, gold and russet surrounded them from head to toe, glinting brightly in the lights of the bedroom. Their mixed magic coated them, tied them together on the most basic level. Intense, intimate, each feather light brush of the linked power ramped her need until her body was in a frenzy of pants, of desperate moans.

The lace of her bra chafed her nipples, beading them to tight points that ached to be sucked on.

Reading the thought across the bond—the bond!—Mason broke away from her mouth, and kissed a path down her neck to her breasts, obliging the unspoken desire.

Her heart pounded and her breath came in short, panting gasps. He surrounded her on every possible avenue—his spicy scent teased her nose, his body pressed against hers, hard to her soft, and his mind . . .

That was wide open.

And there was so much more to process than just simple arousal.

He was turned on, yes, but his consciousness was also filled with affection and love and nervousness. He wanted to make this good, didn't want to hurt her.

On the flip side, he could feel everything she experienced. *Her* desire, her love, her anxiousness to experience this last thing. It was like looking into one of those mirror-inside-of-a-mirror reflections—a perpetual repetition of cycling emotions.

Awesome. Spectacular. And too much.

"I know," he murmured. "Hold on, Sunshine."

He moved so quickly that her breath caught. One second he was over her breasts, and the next he was between her thighs, her panties torn off in a quick, precise movement. His mouth was on her a heartbeat later, licking, sucking, *kissing*. He used his tongue with wicked persistence, circling her clit, winding her higher, making her head spin. The stubble on his chin and cheeks rubbed against her in a delicious friction. His finger slid through her folds, pressed—

She might have been a virgin, but she wasn't an idiot.

This wasn't just sex. This was . . . perfect.

With a flick of his tongue, he sent her over the edge.

Waves of heat and pleasure filled her limbs, making them heavy and lax. It was as though every single cell in her body had simultaneously tightened, paused on the precipice waiting, desperate for released and then . . .

An explosion.

Lights behind her eyes. Love in her soul.

And she was floating in space.

Eventually, she returned to her body to find Mason lying next to her. He had propped his head up on one palm and was watching her, the fingers of his free hand tracing gentle circles on her bare midriff, sparks of their combined magic drifting over her skin. Somewhere in the flurry, she'd lost her bra, so she was buck naked, but the raw way that he stared at her, the heat in his mind and eyes, made her feel totally comfortable. Her lips twitched when she saw that he still wore the towel and she rolled to her side, reaching for it.

"Wait," he said, grasping her wrist. "We don't have to go any further."

Frustration had her trying to pull her hand free. "Yes," she said, yanking against his grip. "Yes, we do."

"No."

The word was intense enough that it drew Gabby's gaze.

"We *don't*," he said, the earnestness in his expression and mind touching her deeper than she'd ever thought possible.

Because no one—perhaps aside from her father—had ever cared about her so much. Mason could easily take her. She wanted it. He wanted it. Hell, she could barely stand the scalding waves of his arousal that bombarded her mind across the bond.

"You can't undo this, Gabby," he continued. "And I don't want to take something you're not yet willing to part with."

He was such a good man.

Smiling and cupping his cheeks in her palms, she met his gaze steadily. "You're right. I don't *have* to do this. But that isn't the question." She paused, trying to find the right words, wanting him to understand. "I know how this works," she murmured. "I know the consequences. I also know you'll wait as long as necessary. But the thing is, I'm done waiting to live my life."

His breath hitched.

"I love you. I've shared my heart, my mind, my *soul* with you. The only thing left is my body." Her eyes stung. "And it aches—physically aches—with the need to be yours. Please, let me have this, let me *give* you this."

He stayed frozen for one more long moment, his shoulders stiff, every muscle in his body taut.

"And," she said softly. "I've already talked with Suz to get the necessary protection." The doctor had implanted the magical form of birth control earlier that week.

At her words, he let out a long, slow breath and the atmosphere in the room shifted.

"You've thought about this."

"Almost every minute of the last two weeks."

He blinked, lips curving. *"Me, too."*

"I love you."

"You're my heart," he said simply, and then . . . further words were unnecessary. The love and affection pouring across the bond eliminated that need altogether. He placed her hands over his heart then held perfectly still as she explored every inch of his chest, his well-defined abs, and the hard length that was between. His pleasure was a tsunami of sensation and despite having an orgasm that had reduced her to mush mere minutes before, Gabby found her own desire quickly ramping up to match his.

"Enough," he eventually grunted, shooing her hands away. Then, with singular focus, he ramped her into a frenzy of jagged pants, sweat covered skin, and a heart that threatened to pound out of her chest. He kissed *every* part of her, breasts and stomach, thighs and in between. Then he knelt between her legs and waited.

Reaching up and locking her arms around his neck, she pulled him close. His chest rested against hers, their hearts separated only by dual layers of bone and tissue.

In one slow press they were joined. It hurt, but not as badly as she had anticipated. And when he kissed her, began moving in small, gentle strokes, the discomfort was completely forgotten.

Their pleasure was intertwined, each fueling the other's, the steady rhythm taking them both up and *up*. As they climbed, the pace of the strokes increased, faster, harder until . . . they both flew over the edge.

This wave of pleasure was more intense, more meaningful, because it was shared release, duel pinnacles reached, two hearts forever united.

Afterward, she lay in his arms and knew without a doubt that she hadn't made a mistake.

He was forever hers.

"*I love you, Sunshine,*" he thought across the bond before they both fell headlong into sleep.

IT WAS his thrashing that woke her later that evening.

His body trembled and his arms, which were around her waist, tightened uncomfortably.

"Mason?" she asked tentatively, squeezing a hand up the slight space between them to cup his face. "Wake up, you're having a—"

A gasp escaped her when he grabbed both of her arms and pinned them above her head in the tight grip of one hand. His other came up to her neck, compressing so tightly that she immediately struggled for breath. Writhing, trying to extract herself from the pinned position, she spoke in hurried, frantic bursts air. "Mason, it's me. It's Gabby. You're dreaming. You need to let me go—"

The final plea was cut off when his hand tightened further.

Black spots began to flash behind her eyes. She couldn't breathe, couldn't get enough oxygen.

His hazel eyes were unseeing—cold depths of fury, glazed from the nightmare, ensnared by the demons of the past.

"Ma—Mase . . ."

The word trailed off as she used the last of her air.

"*Mason,*" she thought, one last, desperate plea before the blackness swallowed her whole.

THIRTY

Mason

HE BLINKED AWAY THE NIGHTMARE. He'd been dreaming that—

"Mason."

The faltering gasp of his name in his mind pulled him straight into consciousness. Horror flooded him as his eyes cleared, sleep fully dissipated, and he found himself on top of Gabby, one hand pinning her arms above her head, the other squeezing her throat.

"God." He tore himself away from her, half stumbling, half-lurching off the bed.

His knees hit the wood floor hard, but he barely noticed the pain, only the cold terror that possessed him as he watched her black out, the markings from his fingers already blemishing the pale skin of her throat.

Carefully, as though he was touching the most fragile of flower petals, as though his touch might be—no, *was*—toxic, he felt for a pulse.

It was strong, steady. As was her presence in his mind.

She was alive.

But whether she would be *okay* was a completely different story.

"Gabby," he whispered, stroking his fingers down her cheek, brushing the hair back from her forehead. "I'm so sorry."

A long gasp of air passed through her lips and her eyes fluttered.

He pulled his hand back, reaching for the discarded towel on the floor and carefully covering her with it. His own state of undress meant nothing to him.

She was the most important thing in his universe.

Fuck. *Fuck.* He'd thought he'd shed the mantle of the past. He'd promised himself that he would protect Gabby from the Dalshie and every other damn thing in the world, and the single thing he'd thought safe—*himself*—had just proven to be the most dangerous.

Wet, pale brown eyes glittered in the dim light.

The fear within their depths just about killed him.

Unable to stop the movement, he lifted his hand, wanting to hold her, to comfort her in his arms. And though he could feel her attempt to mute the reaction, her flinch was still obvious.

"Mason?" she asked, the question hoarse and so tentative that it was a dagger to his gut.

"God, Gabby, I'm sorry. I—"

"You were having a nightmare," she whispered, clutching at the towel as she fumbled for the blanket.

Slowly, so damn slowly, he reached for the comforter and pulled it over her.

"Yes."

"About Victoria and Jacob."

He nodded.

"And you thought I was . . ." Her raspy voice trailed off.

"I *wasn't* thinking."

"Hey. It's not your fault." He started to protest, but she cut him off with a wave of her hand. "You need to talk to someone." His brows drew into a frown. "To someone who *isn't* me. Someone who can help you deal with the PTSD. Suz or Dante or Francis." She shook her head. "I don't know who. But I do know that this can't happen again. I can't—"

"I won't sleep—"

Her voice went hard as steel. "We've bonded Mason," she said in a rasp that just about killed him. "This connection between us is permanent, but . . . I can't have a time bomb in my bed. If I couldn't feel your mind against mine, I would probably be running for the hills right about now." She sighed, tone gentling. "But I can. I can feel you love me. And I love *you*. I *want* to make this work. But this—" A shudder, her eyes going wet. "I can't be terrified to touch you, to see you transform into my worst nightmare." She swallowed hard. "I need you to find a way to fix it."

When she rose from the bed, he averted his eyes, though he'd already memorized every single one of her curves, each freckle and scar.

He was so in tune with her mind that he could feel the rough abrasion of the denim against her thighs as she tugged on her jeans, the soft weight of the cotton against her shoulders and arms as she tugged her T-shirt over her head.

She hesitated at the edge of the bed. "Tell me what you need, and I'll be *here*. Every step of the way."

This time it was him who flinched away from her touch, who shied away from the intimacy of her mind against his.

She curled her hand back, clutched it to her chest. "I'm not leaving you, Mason. I swear, I'm not," she said into the silence, into what was probably the surge of denial from his end that inundated the bond. "But I *need* this night. Let me have the next hours to remember that what just happened wasn't you. Let me remember. Please."

The soft brush of her lips against his cheek was the last thing he felt before the door closed.

And he was alone.

He let her go, ice threatening to settle into his mind, a cold, comforting weight that would numb him to everything. It would be so easy to let it consume him, to return to the state that had made the last decades easier to bear. So *damned* easy—

Shaking off the sensation, he dressed and navigated the corridors to a familiar door.

Less than a second after his soft knock—a second filled with doubts that he was doing the right thing, a second where uncertainty almost made him turn around—the door flew open.

"Mason?" the voice asked.

With an almost inaudible moan of dismay, he stepped forward and took comfort in his mother's arms.

THIRTY-ONE

Gabby

SHE HURRIED DOWN THE HALLS, thankful it was late enough that they were deserted.

The horror of the last ten minutes rattled around in her mind, overwhelming and frightening. She wondered if she'd done the right thing in stepping back.

Despite the calm front she'd adopted once Mason had fully wakened and the realization of what he'd done had crashed into his consciousness, Gabby was terrified.

Strong fingers closing around her throat. Struggling to be free. Fighting to breath. That had happened before. Had—

A whimper rose up in her throat and she swallowed it down.

That hadn't been Mason—that wasn't the man she loved, the man she shared a soul-deep bond with. Yet even knowing that, how was she supposed to sleep next to him without fearing that same thing would happen again?

Her wrists ached, bruises already appearing to encircle

them, and her throat felt as though she'd swallowed a flame-thrower—

She shook her head.

The physical symptoms weren't nearly as painful as the mental ones.

The bond burned with regret, an inferno of guilt and dismay. It was a throbbing abscess that ate at her resolve.

She hadn't wanted to hurt him by leaving. But at the same time, she needed to take a moment to recenter, to remember that wasn't him, that he wouldn't actually hurt her. Because she'd believed it so readily . . . and now she felt like she wore a necklace of bruises.

He needed help, and she didn't know how to give it to him.

The soft voice startled her.

"Gabrielle?"

Francis.

She froze, literally every single muscle in her body halting her forward motion.

Shame welled up, threatened to make her run and hide—

Hell. No.

Stiffening her shoulders, she rotated and faced him. As he caught a glance of her, his eyes widened in concern. "Oh dear, are you all right?" There wasn't anger in his gaze as she'd half-expected—anger because she'd almost hurt one of his students, anger because she couldn't control her powers—nor disappointment.

The only clear emotion in the depths of his light blue eyes was sympathy.

Surprising herself, she burst into tears.

Strong arms wrapped around her, pulled her close.

He didn't say anything as her tears soaked through the starched cotton of his pale gray button-down and when she'd finally quieted, he took her arm, laced it through his own.

"Mason?" he asked.

Fury flew through her. "It wasn't his fault. He—" She bit back the rest of her words, knowing that ultimately Mason needed to share his truth in his own time.

Francis's face gentled. "Come with me," he murmured.

They walked in silence, weaving through the corridors until they arrived at the infirmary.

"I-uh—" Her feet skittered as she tried to stop from entering. It wasn't logical. It wasn't her fault. It wasn't even Mason's fault. But she still didn't want her friends to see her like this: bruised and upset, bedraggled and with wet cheeks.

She was strong, together, supposed to be able to deal with any of life's crises with a mere shrug of her shoulders.

Her mother had become a Dalshie, had killed her father in front of her.

And Gabby had pressed on.

The men who'd paraded through the trailer, trying to take what wasn't freely given, had made her tentative, but not fragile. She'd fought back.

She'd fought *hard*.

And she'd gotten free.

So why did one incident with Mason make her feel as though her heart would be decimated forever?

"Suz will check you over," Francis said. "That is the first thing."

She started to shake her head then sighed. Because Francis was right. If Mason caught sight of her like this again, it would hurt him, and . . . she didn't want him to hurt.

He needed help. She still loved him.

Those weren't two mutually exclusive things.

Sucking in a deep breath for courage, she opened the door and strode inside. Suz was at the reception desk and glanced up at the sound of them entering.

"Dear God—"

Gabby waved a hand. "Everyone's fine." She shrugged. "Or at least no one's injured critically. I need you to take care of this." Her throat was sore enough that the words were raspy. "Then I need you to take care of Mason."

There was a soft laugh behind her, the faintest of chuckles that came from Francis. His hand touched her shoulder, gave it a light squeeze.

And she didn't flinch, didn't react other than to feel appreciation that he'd been there for her. She *wasn't* broken. This hadn't set her back.

"You'll be okay, Gabby," Francis murmured.

She nodded, turned to face him. "Yes," she said, her chin coming up. "We both will be."

"Good girl," he said, and somehow it wasn't condescending or belittling. It was . . . proud. "Come back to class after you've got this sorted. I have a feeling the earlier factors will no longer be an issue."

Stunned, her lips fell open.

A wave of mischievousness made his face appear younger. "You both needed a push." He smiled. "I'm sorry if I hurt your feelings," he said earnestly, "but I can't help it if you gave me the perfect opportunity."

Probably, she should be pissed.

But . . . this man had given her Mason.

So, no. She wasn't angry. She was beyond grateful. "You're just as much of an intervening busybody as the rest of them," she grumbled, but her lips were threatening to curve.

"Guilty as charged." A beat. "Gabby?"

"Yeah?"

"I'm truly sorry that you were hurt—" A shake of his head. "I didn't anticipate—" His eyes glittered with remorse. "I didn't understand enough, and for that, I'm sorry."

She gripped his hand. "Thank you. For the apology, for the interference. I don't blame you. I don't blame *anyone*. It wasn't him, not truly."

Francis nodded, turned for the door. "I know," he said, "But don't make it too easy on him. He needs to conquer these demons once and for all. Otherwise, he'll never be free of them."

The door closed softly behind him.

Gabby turned to Suz, whose chocolate brown eyes flared orange with fiery glints of frustration.

"I'm going to kill him," the doctor said, closing the distance between them, her tone fierce, her fingers gentle as they carefully brushed the marks on Gabby's neck. "I'll burn his nerves, break every bone in his body—"

"He was asleep," Gabby said and then she spent the next few minutes explaining what happened.

"PTSD." Suz shook her head and cursed. "The stubborn man. How long? What other symptoms?"

"Since Victoria. And none that *I* can see." A shrug. "But it's been two weeks."

Another curse. "I stand corrected. The stubborn, *idiotic* man."

"I don't disagree with you. But . . . can you help him?"

Suz froze for a heartbeat before her hands came up to rest on Gabby's shoulders. "Sweetie, we don't leave our own behind."

"But I thought that after what Mason did—"

"It was wrong," the doctor said. "But also not his fault. Or at least not entirely. If you'd told me that he hurt you intentionally or even *unintentionally* because he was careless, then I'd have him on his ass outside the shield so fast that he wouldn't know what hit him—*with* the broken bones. But he's hurting, he's wounded from the past and we don't let our own suffer—no matter how good they are at hiding it."

Gabby's relief was a heady thing. "Thank you."

"Come on," Suz said. "Let's get you healed so we can figure out what to do about Mason."

"We've bonded."

A smile twitched the doctor's lips. "I can see that."

Gabby paused inside the door of the nearest exam room. "You can?"

"His magic is covering you practically head to toe. Or should I say your *combined* magic is."

"What?" Gabby asked, glancing down. She lifted a hand in front of her face, but it just looked the same as normal. "It *is*? How? What does it look like?"

"You've seen Daughtry and Cody, the way their skin seems to glow with a mix of emerald and violet in the right light." Suz's hands settled around Gabby's neck, slender threads of the doctor's brown magic seeping into her throat and soothing the hurts there. "You've been pixie-dusted my friend, no doubt about it."

Gabby made a face. "I can't decide if I'm thrilled or freaked out."

"I know the feeling," came a voice from behind them. Daughtry. "Mason said you were hurt," she explained at their questioning looks.

"I'm fine," Gabby said as Suz moved onto her wrists.

"Word on the street is that you've bonded," Dee said, hesitating in the doorframe until Gabby gestured her forward.

"Word is right."

Dee snorted, then came around to sit next to Gabby, tone serious. "So why is he acting like he should throw himself on that dagger of his?"

Gabby reached for the tender connection in her mind, the completed bond that was currently riddled with Mason's guilt and horror.

"Because he hurt me," she whispered.

Dee's violet eyes clouded in confusion, which was when Gabby realized that she hadn't seen the marks. Even the small hurts on her wrists were already fully healed.

For a moment, she scrambled to find something to say.

Suz intervened. "He was having a nightmare. Gabby woke him. He reacted instinctually and . . ."

Clarity dawned on Daughtry's face and her hand came up to cover her mouth. "Oh God. He's going to tear himself to pieces."

"He already is," Gabby said. "I've asked him to talk to someone, to get help, but I'm worried. What if at the end of it all he still thinks that he's a danger to me?"

"We'll have to convince him otherwise," Daughtry said. "*After* it's safe for you."

"I'll do what it takes—even if I have to handcuff him to the damn bed so he can't grab me."

Dee's lips twitched. "Kinky, but I like it."

Wholly inappropriate based on the evening's events, but laughter bubbled up in Gabby's throat. She let it come, allowed it to wash over her. Because it felt good to share her burdens, to lighten the load she carried instead of shouldering it alone. She nudged Dee's shoulder, mock-glared. "Shut it, you."

Suz snorted. "Seriously. Only a truly depraved person would have gone there in this situation."

The smile that Daughtry had been trying to hold back broke through. "True. Which is why *you* went there too."

Peals of laughter burst out of all three of them.

Gabby hopped off the exam table and stood. "I love you both, you know that right?"

"Yes," Dee said.

"Damn right, you do," Suz quipped.

More laughter, but this time it was paired with two sets of

arms wrapping around her, squeezing her tight. "We love you, too," Dee murmured.

"My mom was a Dalshie," she whispered into the firm net of comfort. "She killed my father." A sigh to bolster her courage. "Then later, I killed her. I had to. I—"

"We know, sweetie," Suz said gently.

Gabby glanced up in surprise. "Y-you *know*?"

Daughtry nodded. "Well, not everything. But we know enough, we *knew* enough."

Shock coursed through her and she stepped back. "And you wanted to be friends with me anyway?" she asked. "Even though I loved her and tried to protect her memory by not telling anyone? Even though part of me still loves her?"

Daughtry's expression gentled. "Do we need to start talking about mommy issues? I think I have you beat."

Considering that Dee's own mother had been behind a slew of attacks on both the Rengalla and on Daughtry herself, Gabby knew that it was true.

"You survived." Dee crossed her arms over her chest. "You didn't turn. You protected yourself."

"I killed her."

Suz shrugged. "You did what you had to in order to survive. That's it."

Gabby shook her head. "But I didn't tell anyone, I didn't—"

"The LexTals aren't stupid, sweetie, they can look at the scene of a Dalshie attack and know by the ash patterns, by the displaced objects and broken furniture what happened."

"*Everyone* knew?"

"I'm sure not *everyone*. But John told Cody." Dee shrugged and spoke as though it was no big deal that every dirty little secret Gabby had worked so hard to shed was common knowledge. "He can't keep anything from me, and I told Suz because I thought she needed to know."

Gabby looked at her friend. "Weren't you mad that I didn't confide in you?"

"Mad?" Suz shook her head. "Of course not. Just because we're friends doesn't mean you have to tell us everything."

"Somehow I doubt you'd be saying that if it involved dishing about Mason."

Daughtry snorted, flashed Suz a grin. "She has you there."

Suz bumped her shoulder against Dee's. "You're just as bad. Nosy meet meddlesome." The phone rang. "Hang on, I'll be right back."

Gabby's mind raced, trying to soak it in. She'd been prepared—since that revelation in Matilda's quarters—to say fuck off to anyone who disliked her because of her past.

What she hadn't anticipated was that people might have already accepted her without compunction.

What kind of freaky fairytale place had she come to live in?

Daughtry laughed, drawing Gabby out of her thoughts. "That good, huh?"

"What?"

"Your face . . . well, bewildered doesn't begin to cover it."

"I—" Gabby shook her head. "I just can't believe that everyone knows and that it's not a big deal. In my head . . ."

"Can I tell you something someone once told me? Something that really helped me put things into perspective?" Dee's voice had softened and Gabby nodded. "He said that it's not all about me. And he didn't say it to be an asshole—neither am I for the record—but because . . . it was—*is* true. Sometimes things in our mind, our hearts seem insurmountable, but really, it's us holding ourselves back."

She blinked, feeling like she'd been standing beneath a giant church bell as it rang in a bell tower overhead. The noise—the words—resonated through her body with all the reverberation of that giant metal cone.

"So what you're saying," Gabby whispered, "is that the universe doesn't revolve around me?"

Daughtry smiled, nudged her shoulder. "Exactly."

She made a face. "Damn."

"Sucks, huh?"

"Yeah." They both laughed, and a moment later, Gabby asked, "Are you—are you okay with not being the only bonded couple?"

Dee snorted. "Are you kidding me? I love that we share the freak status. Maybe everyone will keep gossiping about you and Mason and leave Cody and me alone."

"Not likely," Suz said, as she walked back into the room.

A mischievous glint came into Dee's purple eyes. "Or . . . we could find Suz a bondmate, so that she can join the ranks."

Suz shook her head firmly. "Don't get any ideas. I don't *need* a man."

"You're dating!" Daughtry mock-frowned. "And you're no fun."

"I'm practical."

"*No* fun," Daughtry repeated.

"Not to make it all about me," Gabby said with a grin, interrupting when their argument further devolved into an exchange of yes's and no's. "But how in the hell are we going to convince Mason that he doesn't need to protect me from himself?"

"He'll come around on his own," Dee said. "The bond doesn't really facilitate separation. Give him a week. Trust me, it won't take longer than that."

"And if he proves to be stubborn?" Suz asked.

Gabby thought that was a pretty pertinent question considering the man had spent over a hundred years denying he had a problem with the past.

"If that's the case, we'll give him a good, hard shove," Daughtry said and slung her arm around Gabby's shoulder.

THIRTY-TWO

Mason

THE LAST TWO weeks had been hell.

He was a complete mess, his separation from the woman he loved more awful than he could have imagined. It was worse because Gabby wanted to be there for him, but he didn't trust himself to be alone with her.

He allowed only minimal contact with others around, and the few hours per day he *did* permit himself to be with her were their own special brand of torture.

Regardless, that time with Gabby was still the best part of his day.

They could talk. He could see her smile, make her laugh. But he didn't dare touch, didn't dare put his hands on her. Not even to eliminate the increasing frustration, the occasional sadness that coated her pale brown eyes.

Despite everything, the bond continued to grow—strengthened by their contact, by their mutual love. It withstood the shame and guilt that continued to eat at his soul.

Well, that was all thanks to Gabby—her determination to "save" him.

He would have preferred to leave the Colony altogether, to take his screwed-up self elsewhere until he was certain he couldn't hurt her again.

But they were bonded and if they didn't nuture their connection, the bond would wither. Would die. Gabby would become mortal and lose the powers she'd only begun to control.

It was the hardest thing he'd ever done—staying after what had happened. Staying despite knowing that he'd hurt her, knowing that she was sad because of him—

Knowing his hands had squeezed her delicate throat. That he'd bruised her. Frightened her.

That had been more than enough motivation for him to talk to someone.

Or *someones* because he'd confided in his mother, who'd encouraged him to discuss the problem with Dante. His boss had recommended approaching Suz and Francis and even Tyler for help. Now the entire Colony knew he was seriously fucked up, that he had PTSD. That he'd injured Gabby.

Even worse was that not one person looked at him with contempt.

He deserved to be ostracized, to be viewed with disgust, not considered with sympathy.

He'd hurt his bondmate.

That was unforgiveable.

Yes, he understood that it wasn't really him who'd hurt her, that even though his hands had been around her neck, he hadn't been aware of his actions.

That it had been the nightmare speaking.

The rest of him could still feel her soft skin beneath his fingers, still feel the cold rage within his body as he'd awakened.

And *that* was the problem.

"You need to get over yourself." Tyler's voice surprised him. Mason hadn't realized that anyone had disturbed the solitude he'd sought within the armory.

He set the gun down on the counter, focused on the target he'd been obliterating. His cluster was a little to the left. He needed to fix that, to hit the heart every time. "Go away."

"It's not your fault."

He snorted.

"I felt your mind, Mase. I know what when down."

His chin hit his chest. "I had my hands on her neck. That —you—"

"You've gotten help," Tyler said. "I've taken the nightmare from your mind—"

"You don't understand!" Mason turned, his hands clenched into fists.

"Dude," Tyler said. "Turn that aggression down and focus on the mess that is your mind. This guilt is eating you alive."

It was what everyone had been saying the last weeks, and it wasn't any easier to swallow the hundredth time. Hot rage was simmering within him, fury at the situation, at *himself*—that he couldn't be the man Gabby needed—and burst to the surface. With a frustrated snarl, Mason punched the wall.

Good old Mason logic. Punch shit. Shoot shit. Feel better.

Except, he didn't.

Pain exploded in his hand, but it was nothing compared to the agony in his soul. To the torture of being separated from Gabby.

It was impossible to hold himself away from her.

It was impossible to trust himself near her.

Yet part of him couldn't stifle the hope. Because Tyler *had* removed the nightmare, Francis had given him some mental exercises to center him, to come to terms with the memories, Suz had scanned him brain to make sure there wasn't anything deeper wrong with him, and . . . he'd been sleeping. But was ten days nightmare-free long enough that he could trust himself with her?

Could he *ever* trust himself?

It would only take one dream, one flick of his wrist, and he could kill her as sure as the Dalshie had killed Victoria and Jacob. He—

"That was stupid," Tyler said.

Stupid. Yeah, no kidding. Except Tyler was talking about his hand and Mason was talking about everything else.

He shook his aching fist, felt the hot blood drip down his knuckles, and scented the tang of iron in the air.

"You know I'm not healing that," Tyler said with a nod at the injured limb. "I can't heal stupid."

Mason pulled off his shirt and wrapped it around his hand. "Reading that loud and clear," he muttered.

"I'm not talking about the hand."

Great. Another talk. Another attempt at persuading him to put everything aside and be with Gabby.

"I know."

Silence fell. There were a lot of things that Mason wanted to get off his chest, but he'd already exposed so much of himself to Gabby, to his friends, that he didn't think he could stand to make himself any more vulnerable.

"You know you're good man, right?" Tyler finally asked.

There was the crux of his problem.

Because he'd *thought* himself a good man.

Until he'd had his hand around Gabby's throat. Because . . . nightmare or not, it had been *him*. Some piece of him was capable of hurting her and until that part was fully eradicated he wouldn't trust himself with Gabby.

No matter the agony.

"I'm—"

"*Mason!*"

Gabby's frantic mental voice cut through the layers of agony and hopelessness surrounding his mind. The fear sliced him right down to his soul.

He tried to teleport to her . . . and came against a brick well in his mind. He couldn't. He couldn't get to her.

"What's the—?" Tyler started to ask.

Mason was running before he'd even processed he was moving. His feet ate through the corridors, pounded up the stairs and out the front door.

Because Gabby wasn't safe. She was outside the shield.

He didn't question why the layer of magic that protected the Colony parted before he'd even reached it. The only thoughts that were running through his mind were how quickly he could get to her, how hurt she might be, and how much magic he would need when he got to her.

"*Gabby,*" he thought for the hundredth time in the last few minutes, trying to rouse her and feeling nothing in returned. She'd screamed his name and then nothing. Her mind was a brick wall, impenetrable to his hails.

The only thing he could sense was her direction and that she was alive.

Accelerating using his magic, Mason flew across the miles that separated them. He could only pray he would get there in time. Up he went, the trees a blur, the shield and Colony fading into the background.

His stomach clenched in horror when he realized where she was.

The waterfalls.

Fuck. Flying down the right fork of the trail, he heard the pounding of the water against the rocks, felt the mist in the air, smelled the wet stone.

A heartbeat later, he was on the outcropping of bare granite, the cascade of water deafening.

His gaze swung from side to side, frantically searching.

There!

She was just feet from the cliff. He ran over, reached out—

"Stop!" she yelled over the noise.

Feet skidding to a halt, he obliged, less than five feet separating them. "Are you hurt?" he called.

"No!" She shook her head, but then the bond opened up—filled him with the torrent of her emotions, her pain, her hope, her despair—and she thought to him, *"Yes."* Her hand came up to cover her heart. *"I hurt so much here."*

Panic was replaced by guilty agony. "I can't, Sunshine. I'm not—"

"Safe?" she asked. "You're my chance at forever. I *need* you."

She was too close to the falls, too close to the slick edge of granite.

He took a step toward her. "Come here."

"No." She skittered back another foot. "Not until you promise, not until you swear you won't let fear rule you."

"It's not that easy."

"It *is.*"

He was already shaking his head, ready to tell her that it wasn't, when she slipped.

Her scream pierced through the air as she plummeted over the edge.

THIRTY-THREE

Gabby

SHE LET out a very choice curse word as she fell.

It wasn't part of the plan for her to fall off the damn cliff.

Again.

She'd meant to get him isolated, separate enough that he would have to face her instead of avoiding her—instead of using almost every other person in the Colony like a human shield as he'd been doing during their time together. She was getting a decidedly prison-like-conjugal feel from those unsatisfying daily visits. The time spent together might be preventing the bond from breaking, but it wasn't making things better for either of them.

Still, falling off the freaking edge of the cliff wasn't her idea of smart. If he didn't get to her in time she was—

Toast.

Or that was what she *had* been thinking when a pair of strong arms encircled her waist.

Water soaked them both, pounded painfully against their skin, as they rose slowly into the sky.

They didn't speak until they were on the top of the falls.

"Mason, I—"

"You idiot woman!" he shouted, fury making every muscle in his body as taut as steel. "What were you thinking jumping off that cliff? What if I hadn't been able to get to you in time? What if—?"

"I didn't jump," she said, shoving at his arms. "I'm not *that* stupid! It was an accident!"

"People don't fall off the same cliff twice by *accident*!"

Finally succeeding in freeing herself, she plunked her hands on her hips, angry even though she'd been thinking the same thing. "I didn't fall the first time. I was *pushed*." She glared. "*This* time, I slipped."

"It was stupid to be so close."

"It was stupid to avoid me for so long," she countered. "I wouldn't even *be* here if you weren't so monumentally stubborn." Her hands dropped to her sides. "Why can't you just give in and admit that you can't live without me?"

"I can't."

The words cut at her, sliced her to the quick. She couldn't have heard that correctly. "You can't? You. Can't?" she repeated like an idiot. "But . . ."

"Sunshine, I can't *live* without you, but I can't risk hurting you," he said. "That's why I've been getting help. Why I've talked to almost every damn person in the Colony."

"Not that it makes a difference," she muttered. "I know you're not convinced that you're safe to be around me."

"That's true."

"And you won't sleep with me again until you're sure."

"That's also true."

A shriek of frustration escaped her. "That's not fair, Mason. I need you. I hurt without you. I want to *be* with you. Doesn't that count for anything?"

He opened his mouth, but she waved him off. "Can't we take precautions? You're not the only person in the universe with PTSD, you know? We can handcuff you to the bed. I can talk to you across the bond instead of shaking you awake. Hell, Francis and Dante can recommend a therapist if you don't think Tyler is helping."

At the end of her speech, she paused, waiting for him to say something, anything, even to tell her she was dead wrong.

Instead, he said nothing.

His mind was tangled, his emotions and expression unreadable.

All of the hope she'd held evaporated, and the pain of separation increased tenfold. She should have known that nothing she could say would make a bit of difference. Because Mason wanted the one hundred percent guarantee he would never hurt her again.

And that just didn't exist.

Striding away, her eyes stinging, misery swelling within her, she tried to tell herself to be patient. It had only been a few weeks. It would get better and—

It didn't work.

She'd spent so long hiding from life that to be teased with only a few days of truly living it, of finally feeling and loving and experiencing everything she'd only ever hoped for—

Well, it sucked. Big time.

Her wet jeans abraded her thighs and made her movements jerky. Her sneakers slid slightly on the damp granite.

Gabby sighed. This might suck, but it wasn't the end of the world.

Swiping away a traitorous tear, she started to turn back to Mason, ready to tell him that she loved him, and would stop pushing. That someday she hoped he would find the peace he sought and would fully come back to her.

"You want to handcuff me to the bed?" Amusement coursed across the bond. "Didn't know you were into the kink, Sunshine."

"I—"

He appeared right in front of her, ran his fingers over her cheekbone. She gasped in surprise, her feet slipping out from beneath her, and she hit with a bone-jarring *thud*, her hands scrabbling for something to slow her because . . . she was sliding toward the edge of the waterfall.

For the third fucking time.

He grabbed her, swept her up into his arms, and yanked her to the trees before she even had the chance to scream.

"Woman," he said, panting, sweat and water dripping down his forehead, his arms still tight around her waist. "What the hell do you think you're doing?"

"Nothing!" she yelled. "I push and it doesn't help. I give and you stay distant." She tossed up her hands. "What the fuck do you *want* from me?"

He went perfectly still for one long heartbeat of time.

Something monumental was aligning in his mind, and the reverberation of that realization pounded across the bond.

"I want *everything*," he whispered, his arms contracting, pulling her tight against him. "Good God, Gabby, I'm an idiot."

Dumbfounded, she shrugged.

He cursed again then released her, letting her find her feet before one palm came up to cup her cheek. "I could have lost you. From a stupid accident. If I wasn't here"—he shoved a hand through his hair—"I know life is too damned short. I know how easy it is to lose someone you love. I *know* and I've still been so stupid."

"What are you saying?" she asked, hopeful and yet so damned scared.

"The same thing everyone has tried to drill into my stubborn ass brain a hundred times." He pushed back her damp bangs and pressed a kiss to her forehead. "But I couldn't believe it. No, *I* had to pretend that I was the exception, that I—"

"Mason!" she said, cutting off the flow of words. "*What are you saying?*"

"I'm saying I'm sorry I'm an idiot. I'm sorry I hurt you by staying away." His voice cracked. "I spent a century hiding from emotions. Then I met you and was able to feel again. I can't just throw that away. I can't throw *you* away, Sunshine. You mean too much."

Her heart thudded, her throat contracted. "You promise?" she asked, touching the bond with her mind, trying to ascertain how sure he was.

"It's more than a promise," he said. "It's the damned truth. I don't want to lose you because of a slip." He raised his other palm to her face. His eyes, his mind were filled with such earnestness that her uncertainty faded away. "And God forbid, if something happens, I don't want to regret not having more time with you."

"I—" She shook her head. "But why now? What's changed in the last five minutes?"

"It's simple"—his lips twitched—"I just can't bear to watch you throw yourself off that cliff in another attempt to get me to pay attention."

Outrage bubbled in her blood. "I—"

"I love you," he murmured and pressed his mouth to hers, proceeding to kiss the irritation right out of her. "I can't promise you I won't screw up, Sunshine," he said after he'd finally pulled back, their hearts galloping, their minds and bodies firmly meshed. "But I'm done with throwing away our time together."

"And if you have another nightmare?" she asked.

"I haven't had any since I talked to Tyler the first time. But if they come back, rouse me through the bond. I'll know it's you." He smiled and thought to her, *"I'll trust in the bond, have faith that I'd know you even in the deepest, darkest circle of hell."*

"Well," she murmured. "That's a start."

Mason laughed and pulled her into his arms. "Let's get you away from these falls."

"No argument there."

As they walked down the trail, Gabby knew that though they'd crossed the first hurdle, there would be more. Their relationship was new, still growing and developing into what it would one day become.

But what she had faith in now was that their bond ran deeper than fear. That so long as one of them was willing to fight for the other, then nothing—the past, the demons that masqueraded as nightmares, even slippery-as-hell waterfalls—would ever be able to separate them.

Love had stitched them together, soul to soul, magic to magic, mind to mind.

Nothing could sever those ties.

"Promise me that you'll never go there by yourself," Mason said as they approached the Colony.

Considering her track record, she didn't argue.

"I promise," she said, love filling her to near bursting. "I wouldn't jump out of a plane without a parachute and I wouldn't risk living without the other half of my heart.

IN FLAMES

Suz

ANOTHER DATE.

Another loser.

Sighing, she waited long enough so the man—said loser—would have vacated the hallway then slipped out of her room and made her way to the infirmary.

It was empty, but she could always find something to do.

And, if she waited long enough, someone would get hurt and she'd have something to do, something that wasn't sitting around being jealous because her friends were ridiculously happy and bonded and . . . she was dating losers.

Which wasn't *entirely* fair.

The Rengalla she'd gone out with that evening was a nice man.

Just not the one for her.

And, if she were being completely honest, he was a little borning.

As her life had been . . . for decades.

Nearly a hundred years old, she'd lived through medical and

technological advancements, she'd lived through wars and loss, and . . . she was bored out of her mind.

She wanted excitement.

She wanted to feel something, *anything* aside from this heavy weight sitting on her chest.

The one that told her she was missing out, missing something.

Not doing enough. Not helping enough. Not living—

Enough.

Yes, that was a trend with her.

Lonely.

That was also a trend. Because as much as the men she'd dated had waxed poetic about liking strong women, that hadn't actually come to fruition, especially when she was pulled into the infirmary because someone had broken their leg, or burned their arm, or because a baby had decidedly to make an untimely arrival.

Then they realized that dating the Rengalla's top healer wasn't all fun and games.

Then . . . they went away.

And circling back to lonely. And horny.

Because that was the crux of it, too. She was tired of her hand and her vibrator. She wanted an orgasm courtesy of someone else. She wanted a man to look at her with desire, to want, to *need* her.

Like Dee had.

Like Gabby had.

Like she would probably *never* have.

Sighing, she grabbed the doorknob, started to push into the infirmary. Maybe she wouldn't ever bond, or have a man devoted to her like her friends did, "But, is it too much for me to have just *one* night of hot sex?"

"Pent up, Suzie girl?"

That voice.

Liquid honey down her spine, heat drifting between her thighs, desire making the tips of her fingers itch—

To loose her magic, to wipe that smirk off his gorgeous face.

To . . . wrap in the strands of his deep brown hair and yank his head down for a kiss.

She let go of the knob and turned to face Graham.

Cocky, funny Graham.

Who *everyone* liked. Who was nice to every Rengalla big and small.

Every Rengalla except for her.

Her he liked to torment.

She couldn't stand the man. He was too arrogant by half, and never failed to infuriate her. But he wasn't dating anyone, and clearly after that evening, she wasn't either.

And . . . she wanted him, had spent years wanting him.

She stepped toward him, close enough to smell him—all damp forest floor and warm summer sunshine—closer enough to feel the heat from his body, sense his strength in the hard planes of his body.

"You offering to help me out?" she asked, taking another step, her breasts brushing against his chest.

A muscle ticked in his jaw. "Suz," he muttered, putting some distance between them. "Don't be ridiculous."

Hurt. God, it sliced right through her, tore at her insides.

Not even the man who'd slept with half the single women in the Colony wanted her.

Cool.

She forced a laugh, her eyes burning. So stupid. "Right," she said and spun around, reached for the knob. "I'm busy. Now go away."

"Wait." He grabbed her arm.

She shook him off, pushed into the place that had become

her sanctuary. Maybe there were some bandages to organize, some charts to file—

Click.

That wasn't the sound of the door closing.

Rather, it was the sound of the door *locking*.

On a gasp, she spun around.

Graham was there, eyes hot as he stepped away from the door. "So little Suzie girl is all pent up," he said, the words sending a shiver down her spine. He crowded into her. "She needs help scratching an itch—"

She lifted her chin. "Go to he—"

He kissed her.

IN FLAMES

Into Flames is coming January 25th, 2021. Preorder your copy
at www.books2read.com/inflames

ALSO BY ELISE FABER

Billionaire's Club (all stand alone)

Bad Night Stand

Bad Breakup

Bad Husband

Bad Hookup

Bad Divorce

Bad Fiancé

Bad Boyfriend

Bad Blind Date

Bad Wedding

Bad Engagement

Bad Bridesmaid (March 1st, 2021)

Gold Hockey (all stand alone)

Blocked

Backhand

Boarding

Benched

Breakaway

Breakout

Checked

Coasting

Centered

Charging (December 28th, 2020)

Caged (March 2021)

Love, Action, Camera (*all stand alone*)

Dotted Line

Action Shot

Close-Up

End Scene

Meet Cute (April 5th, 2021)

Love After Midnight (**all stand alone**)

Rum And Notes

Virgin Daiquiri

On The Rocks

Sex On The Seats (April 26th, 2021)

Life Sucks Series (**all stand alone**)

Train Wreck

Hot Mess

Dumpster Fire (February 15th, 2021)

Roosevelt Ranch Series (**all stand alone, series complete**)

Disaster at Roosevelt Ranch

Heartbreak at Roosevelt Ranch

Collision at Roosevelt Ranch

Regret at Roosevelt Ranch

Desire at Roosevelt Ranch

Phoenix Series (read in order)

Phoenix Rising

Dark Phoenix

Phoenix Freed

Phoenix: LexTal Chronicles (rereleasing soon, stand alone, Phoenix world)

From Ashes

In Flames (January 25th, 2021)

To Smoke

KTS Series

Fire and Ice (Hurt Anthology, stand alone)

Riding The Edge (December 7th, 2020)

Stand Alones

Someday, Maybe (YA)

ABOUT THE AUTHOR

USA Today bestselling author, Elise Faber, loves chocolate, Star Wars, Harry Potter, and hockey (the order depending on the day and how well her team -- the Sharks! -- are playing). She and her husband also play as much hockey as they can squeeze into their schedules, so much so that their typical date night is spent on the ice. Elise changes her hair color more often than some people change their socks, loves sparkly things, and is the mom to two exuberant boys. She lives in Northern California. Connect with her in her Facebook group, the Fabinators or find more information about her books at www.elisefaber.com.

facebook.com/elisefaberauthor

amazon.com/author/elisefaber

bookbub.com/profile/elise-faber

instagram.com/elisefaber

goodreads.com/elisefaber

pinterest.com/elisefaberwrite